BEHEMOTH
A NOVEL ——▶

John Ingelin

To Linda,
Blessings –
John Angel

Clovercroft Publishing

Behemoth

© 2015 by John Ingelin

Published by Clovercroft Publishing,
Franklin, Tennessee.

Published in association with
Larry Carpenter of Christian Book Services, LLC.
www.christianbookservices.com

Cover and Interior Design by Adept Content Solutions

Edited by Bob Irvin

Printed in the United States of America

978-1-942557-07-4

ACKNOWLEDGMENTS

There are two people I must mention. I know it sounds cliché, but this book would not exist if not for their encouragement and support.

First, my good friend Rochelle Hook. After reading a very rough, unfinished draft, she stated, "This needs to get out!" Thanks, Rochelle. It's out.

Second, and most important, my wife Cindy. What a blessing to have someone in your corner who believes in you and is not afraid to ask, "Why are you not writing?"

CONTENTS

CHAPTER ONE

In a time of universal deceit, telling the truth becomes a revolutionary act.

—George Orwell[1]

Picking up speed, Ethan leaned over his handlebars, straining to see through the morning fog that still hung in the air. Jagged boulders pressed hard along one side, massive trees on the other. The cool, damp air intensified the heavy aroma of cedar. Water from low-hanging branches drenched Ethan's back and ran down his arms. His slippery hands fought for control of his mountain bike as the trail became a tangle of twisted roots. His legs continued to pump furiously as he drove straight through a stream that rushed across the trail. Ethan knew he was going too fast on the punishing trail, but he never considered using his brakes. He felt powerful and alive, as though he was chasing—or being chased by—something wild. Perhaps he was unleashing some deep primal instinct. But Ethan knew it wasn't just adrenaline and muscle that fueled his ferocity. He knew that it was anger.

Ethan was heading toward Hobbs Point, the biggest housing development in the county. The closer he got, the more his anger grew. A thousand acres of rolling hills were being torn up to build monstrous, self-indulgent houses. But these McMansions were not the source of Ethan's uncontrollable rage. This rage was spurred by the company in charge of the massive project: the one and only David Booker Construction Company.

This particular David Booker was a talented local man who had transformed his small struggling construction company into an enormous success. Normally, Ethan would respect and admire such a man. However, Ethan knew David Booker beyond his role as owner of a thriving construction company.

David Booker was Ethan's father.

Even though Ethan was racing toward Hobbs Point, he had no desire to actually see his father. After all the things his father had done, he should be racing away. Yet here he was, as if drawn by some unknown force.

A tiny part of Ethan was proud of his father. The company's success was due primarily to his father. Unfortunately, David Booker's character did not match his business expertise. Two years ago he had walked out on his wife and son. Ethan was fifteen at the time, and never understood why. All he knew was that his father had turned his back on a teenage son who worshiped him and a wife who loved him. Ethan had rarely seen him since. He had no desire to spend time with someone he despised.

Hobbs Point was still about a half mile away. Ethan knew he should be resting before tonight's baseball game, but sitting still was not an option. Ethan needed an escape from his anger, if only for a couple of hours. He tried hard to keep it hidden beneath the surface; however, after two long years that anger remained. Now that the David Booker Construction Company was back in town, the rage resurfaced. Riding his bike hard was the perfect outlet. Concentrating on the treacherous path through the woods helped him forget. *So why did he continue to race toward his dad?*

Above the treetops, Ethan could see mushrooming plumes of smoke and could hear the low rumble of heavy equipment. Hobbs Point was just ahead. *What was he doing here? What did he expect to accomplish? Deep down, did he want to yell at his dad, even from a distance?* He turned his focus back to the trail as it funneled down through a narrow chute between a thick clump of trees and then over a crest. The trail disappeared beyond the crest, but Ethan knew it would then open up directly onto a large open meadow. As he got closer and closer to the construction site, his resentment for his dad grew and grew. Ethan gathered speed as he drove straight through the funnel and soared over the crest.

Bulldozers had scraped away the entire meadow. Ethan was not prepared for the drop. He pitched forward, crashing straight down on a pile of rocks and gravel, slamming his chest on his handlebars before flipping all the way over and landing flat on his back. Ethan lay sprawled out on a pile of rubble. For a while he didn't move as he waited for his breath to return and his head to clear. Slowly he opened his eyes and stared up at the gray sky. A minor ache in his head was rapidly becoming an intense throb. He sat up and gently took off his helmet, which was cracked nearly in two. Ethan paused to thank his mom for insisting that he always wear it. The burning sensation coming from his knee made sense considering the amount of blood oozing out and running down his shin. Surprisingly, Ethan found no other significant damage—until he noticed his bike. The front rim was mangled, and the front fork was crushed.

Ethan decided to test his knee as he contemplated the long walk home. No way would he let his father see him like this. He stood up and took one tiny step. The gash actually looked worse than it really was. He gingerly made his way across the rubble and grabbed the water bottle from his broken bike. He flushed most of the gravel out of his knee, saving a bit of water to drink. Ethan grimaced when he thought about carrying his bike all the way back home on a torn-up knee. He had no other choice. He couldn't ask his dad for help, nor could he leave the bike behind for his dad to find later. Ethan looked across at the development. Off in the distance, on the highest point, sat a construction trailer with the name David Booker Construction emblazoned in large red letters across the front.

Ethan drew a deep breath into his sore chest, put a hand on his throbbing forehead, and stared at his bloody knee. *Perfect. Can't even get near the guy without getting hurt.*

∞ ∞ ∞ ∞ ∞ ∞ ∞

A few days later at Hobbs Point, a young worker jumped off a bulldozer and ran to David Booker's side. "Boss, this is all wrong. There's no way I should be pushing up dirt for a pond right here. All the drainage from that northern slope will drain right to this very spot. Plus, it won't get any shade, so the sun will turn that pond into algae soup before the middle of June."

David smiled at the young worker. "You're absolutely right, Marty."

"Well, yeah. Of course, I am. So what are we going to do about it?"

"We're going to build a pond right there," David said, not stopping so much as to pause.

Marty didn't say a word.

"This whole development," continued David, "will be inhabited by people with a great deal of money, and the wealthiest one of the bunch, Mr. J. Sterner of Sterner Broadcasting, owns this five-acre section. What Mr. Sterner wants, Mr. Sterner gets, and he wants an unobstructed view of the sunset over his half-acre pond, right there."

"Well, good for him," said the young worker. "Only it ain't gonna work."

"It'll work, Marty. I've already ordered extra filtration and a massive aeration system."

"Wow. I guess he's going to owe you a favor," Marty said.

"Yeah, I guess he will." David looked out at the huge lot with just a bit of envy. "But I'm not going to owe you for any overtime. Jump back on that bulldozer, and dig that pond."

Marty shook his head as he climbed back into the cab of the massive machine. Smoke billowed into the sky as he lowered the blade and rumbled forward.

David noticed Bill standing nearby. Not only was Bill the on-site foreman, he and David were good friends.

"Hey, Bill. Did you see the game last night?"

"Sure did, David. Great game," Bill said, glancing from time to time at the clipboard he carried.

"Well, how'd Ethan do?"

"You know, my son Josh plays on that team too—so, thanks for asking. Josh struck out three times, but he did get on base when he was hit by a pitch. If you ask me, I'd say he leaned into it. Caught it on the elbow. But don't worry, I think he'll be OK."

David sighed as Bill made him wait while he checked his clipboard again. Bill delayed a moment longer, annoying his old friend. "OK, OK. Ethan smashed two doubles. He scored the winning run on a squeeze play. You know, David, since you're back in town, you shoulda been there."

"I can't, Bill. You know it would be a bad scene."

"Look, David, we all make mistakes. Maybe not as big and dumb as yours. You should just call her. I know you want to. This is a perfect opportunity. You're going to be in town for six months. You haven't been to the casino for over a year. You can't tell me you're just going to ignore Abi and Ethan for that long."

David hung his head. "Thanks for the report, Bill. Oh, and tell Josh to take those bean balls on his shoulder, not the elbow."

"Great advice. Thanks, Boss."

As David headed back to his trailer, an odd noise stopped him in his tracks. He looked at Marty, who had started carving out the pond. His bulldozer had just struck something. Dozers hit boulders just beneath the surface all the time. They are constructed for just that possibility. Their blades are five-inch-thick hardened carbon steel. But this noise was unusual, perhaps a different pitch. The bulldozer now had David's full attention. Marty backed up ten feet, dropped the blade, and once again pushed ahead. Even with all the noise of the other heavy equipment at the site, David once again heard the odd clunk. This time a whitish-gray object erupted from the pile of rubble and dirt pushed by the blade.

David ran toward the bulldozer waving his arms. "Hey! Marty! Shut it down! Shut it down!"

Marty turned off the dozer and leaned out of the cab. "What's up, Boss? What is it?"

David picked up one of the smaller grayish-white pieces. "You're done digging here today. Looks like you hit the mother lode."

Marty looked confused. "The mother lode of what?"

"Fossils," David said. "These are fossils. I would guess some sort of dinosaur bones."

"That's right. Your wife is like one of those bone diggers, a . . . a . . . "

"Paleontologist," said David. "And you mean ex-wife."

David put two fingers in his mouth and whistled loudly to his foreman. "Bill! Come here and bring your clipboard."

Bill headed over, walking as quickly as he could, holding his hard hat so it wouldn't fly off as he did. "What's up?"

"I need you to secure this area and call the local university. That's proper procedure when something like this happens. We've got a dinosaur on our hands."

"You've gotta be kidding. That's going to delay our schedule on this section. Mr. Sterner is not going to be happy."

David poked at one of the larger bones with his foot. "Mr. Sterner will have to live with a short delay. There's nothing we can do about it."

Bill picked up a bone slightly larger than a baseball bat and held it out to David. "Hey, now you have a perfect reason to call Abi."

"Nah. She doesn't do this anymore. Besides, I'm sure this is just run-of-the-mill fossil stuff. Nothing unusual . . ." David's voice trailed off as he turned the bone over. Something unusual caught his eye. "You know, maybe I will give her a call."

As David carried the fossil back to his trailer, he once again surveyed the entire expanse spread out before him. Winning the Hobbs Point bid solidified his company as one of the largest in Oregon. Professionally, he was at the top of his game. He could look at an undeveloped parcel and envision a perfect neighborhood. He could shape and manipulate the earth in beautiful ways, not just complementing the topography, but improving it. At times he felt like God.

Unfortunately, his personal life was a different matter. With his newfound wealth he drank too much, gambled too much, and for some reason he still didn't fully understand, left his wife of eighteen years for a much younger, extremely attractive stockbroker he had met in a bar. Leaving his wife Abi also meant leaving his son Ethan. Without a doubt, it was the biggest mistake he had ever made.

He needed the perfect excuse to call his ex-wife. Now he held it in his hands.

∞ ∞ ∞ ∞ ∞ ∞ ∞

Ethan let the screen door slap loudly behind him as he stomped into the house. "I'm home," he said as he strode quickly past the kitchen, where his mom was busy cutting up vegetables next to the sink.

"No kidding," she said.

Ethan was already halfway up the stairs when his mother's cell phone rang.

"Ethan, can you get that? It's on the counter!" she shouted.

Annoyed, he turned himself around, as though answering her phone was some massive undertaking, and clomped back down the stairs. He snatched the phone and hit the slider to answer it on the fifth ring.

"Hello?"

"Ethan, this is your dad."

His frustration at having to answer the phone was now complete. Ethan was instantly reminded of the pain his dad had caused, not to mention his lingering headache and his scabby knee. He started to hang up.

"Wait, wait! This is important," his father shouted.

Ethan nearly laughed to himself. *Good for you, Dad—you knew I was going to end the call on you. Of course, any fool would have guessed that.*

Ethan held the phone back to his ear without saying anything.

"I need to tell your mother something. At the site today we hit some dinosaur bones."

"Who is it?" his mother asked. Late in the afternoon, and working, she had a tired look—and tired voice.

"No one important, Mom." Ethan intended his comment to sting. The pause on the end of the line confirmed that it worked.

Ethan's dad tried again. "I really think your mom should look at this."

Ethan pressed the attack. "Are you sure you didn't stumble onto a dead cow?" As much as Ethan enjoyed shooting barbs through the phone, his headache suddenly returned with a vengeance. Ethan knew he was treating his dad like dirt. Even *he* knew it was an awful thing—but a large part of him enjoyed it.

David kept his voice calm. "Like I said, I need to talk to your mother."

"Dead cow?" his mom asked as she took the phone from her son, glancing from Ethan over to the wall as she answered. "Who is this?"

Ethan watched his mother's face as she realized who was on the phone. Her eyes widened, her mouth opened slightly, and she stood up taller. For a moment, it seemed as though she was excited. *Unbelievable.*

She looked at Ethan. "Yes, I'm sure you know the difference between a dead cow and a dinosaur bone. OK, so you think you dug up a fossil. Fine. This kind of thing happens more often than you might think. I assume you know the procedure. There are laws, David. You have to deliver the bones to the scientific community. But first you must completely secure the area."

Ethan was pleased that his mother's initial thrill at hearing her ex-husband's voice had been replaced by a far more appropriate attitude.

"No, I don't need to see them," she continued. "I don't do field work anymore. Besides, I'm sure you can find someone else."

That was good, Mom. Now hang up. But to Ethan's complete annoyance, his mother kept listening.

"What do you mean 'unusual'?" she said. "David, is this some kind of a lame scheme of yours now that you're back in town? Did your hot stockbroker find a different bar where she can hang out?"

Ethan smiled. *Good one, Mom.*

"Sorry, David. I shouldn't have said that." She paused, taking a breath. "OK, tell me more about this fossil."

What? Ethan could not believe it. *This is absurd, Mom. You should not be the one apologizing! Not now, not ever!*

"Fair enough. I'll meet you at Hobbs Point later." His mom hung up and looked at Ethan. "Apparently your father dug up a fossil."

"Yeah . . . maybe."

"Your father said there was something unusual about it, but he didn't want to discuss it on the phone."

Ethan's head began to throb once more. He could feel his face getting red.

"If you have something to say, Ethan, say it."

Ethan started pacing, searching for the right words. "Two years ago. Just two years ago that man stabbed us in the heart. Since then we have done everything we can to put the pain behind us. Now, after one phone call, you're willing to forget all that. He's just pushing your buttons, Mom. Please, tell me you're not that gullible."

"It's a fossil, Ethan. Believe me, this has nothing to do with your father."

Ethan's eyes narrowed. "We've spent the last two years looking to the future. I don't want to go backwards, Mom. I won't see you get hurt again."

"I appreciate that, Ethan. But I'm going to see the fossil."

∞ ∞ ∞ ∞ ∞ ∞ ∞

Ethan found it difficult to comprehend that his mother was going to see his father. He gave in to her resolve on the condition that they go together. No way did Ethan want her going alone. Unfortunately, he had to call his friend Geneva and cancel their date. Actually, it wasn't really a date. Gen and Ethan had been friends since kindergarten. They were still really good friends and, obviously, friends don't date. Besides, Ethan knew Gen would think him weird if he told her how he really felt about her.

"Who were you talking to?" Ethan's mom asked.

"Just Gen. We were supposed to do something tonight."

"For goodness sake, don't cancel on my account. I'm perfectly capable of seeing David on my own."

"Gen thought it was a good idea that I go with you. If Gen thinks it's a good idea, then it must be a good idea," Ethan answered.

"Good point," said Abi. "But this shouldn't take long. You should have plenty of time later for your date."

"We're just getting together. It isn't like a *date* date."

"A *date* date?" his mom said, eyebrow raised. "Don't be *dumb* dumb, Ethan."

"I guess I would come by that naturally," Ethan said sarcastically. "Speaking of which, Dad is probably waiting for us."

They climbed into Ethan's pride and joy, his '71 Monte Carlo, and headed to Hobbs Point. Ethan could tell that his mother was anxious. If she was nervous, that would be expected. If she was eager, Ethan hoped the fossil was the cause, not his father. Clearly, his mother was intrigued by what had been uncovered. Even though she no longer worked in the field and only taught part time, Ethan knew she still had the bug. She used to tell Ethan that every paleontologist dreams of discovering something extraordinary, something that transforms the way science looks at the world. She also told Ethan a discovery of that type was highly unlikely.

Ethan had only been up to the site once, and that was earlier in the day, when he crashed his mountain bike, but he knew where to find his dad. He would be in the trailer perched on the high point overlooking the operation. He did not disappoint. David was waiting for Abi outside the trailer and was obviously surprised to see his son.

Ethan could not take his eyes off his dad. How weird to see him after all this time. He looked totally familiar—and yet totally foreign all at the same time. This was the dad who taught him how to play ball and catch fish. But this was the same dad who ripped his family to pieces in order to follow his own selfish desires. *How could one man's character crumble so quickly after a taste of success?*

"Abi, Ethan, I'm so glad you came," David said.

"I'm not here to see you," Ethan said through his rolled-down window. "I'm here for Mom."

David simply nodded and walked to the passenger side of the car. Abi opened the car door and stepped out. Ethan was pleased that his mom did not dress up for the meeting.

She still had on the same blue jeans and sweatshirt she had worn all day.

"OK, where's the site?" she asked the moment David stood next to her.

"It's really nice to see you, Abi," David said.

"The site, David. Where is it?"

"Down past that ridge to the left."

"Fine. Let's go," she said.

"Hold on. The fossil I wanted to show you is here in my office."

"What? You removed a fossil from the area? Even you know better than that, David. The Paleontological Society will be all over you. You guys will be fined big time."

David simply turned and started heading for the trailer. "Probably. Do you want to see it or not?"

Ethan quickly got out of his car and went to his mother. "This isn't right, Mom. Even I know the fossil should still be at the dig site. Let's just go back home."

His mom sighed heavily and looked at her son. "As long as we are here, I might as well see the fossil. You just never know."

Ethan followed his mom and dad into the trailer. The unique odor of the trailer was instantly familiar: a combination of stale coffee, dirt, diesel fuel, and sweat. The walls were covered with topographical maps and calendars. David quickly placed a framed picture on his desk face down. Ethan recognized the frame, although he wondered whose picture was inside. The fossil was lying haphazardly on top of his desk. Abi walked over and looked at it briefly.

"David, it's clearly a femur, most likely from an allosaurus," she said. "Very nice, but more than fifty of these already exist in museums around the world. Thank you for calling me."

With that she turned to Ethan. "Let's go home."

Ethan could feel her disappointment. He was not certain whether his mother was simply disappointed with the fossil or disappointed with herself that she had been so easily manipulated.

David took a step toward Abi and smiled. "Don't go just yet. First, turn it over."

Even to Ethan this seemed a ridiculous request. *Why would the other side of a fossil be more interesting?* His mom took a deep breath, rolled her eyes, and turned back to the desk. This time she picked up the bone and slowly turned it over in her hands. Her eyes widened. She quickly carried it to a large drafting table, sweeping all the drawings on it to the floor. Ethan leaned around his mother, straining to see what might have caused such a reaction. He could see an unusual black rock that appeared to be stuck into the bone.

She leaned in close. "Magnifying glass," she mumbled, to no one in particular, her hand thrust out like a surgeon awaiting his scalpel.

David handed her one that he obviously had ready. Minutes passed without a word from his mom as she examined every inch of the fossil. Finally, her face flushed, she looked up at her ex-husband.

"Like I said, thanks for calling me." She gave him a big smile and went right back to studying the bone.

CHAPTER TWO

———➤

Truth will ultimately prevail where there is pains taken to bring it to light.

—George Washington

As soon as Ethan left the house on his "date," Abigail Booker immediately drove to the far side of town. Clutching a bundle in her arms, she walked eagerly up the three cracked cement steps to the front door of a small old house. With obvious excitement, she knocked rapidly on the faded wood door.

A slightly nervous voice called out from inside. "Who is it?"

"Joseph. It's me. Abigail. Dr. Booker?"

After a short pause, Abi heard a lengthy series of clicking and clunking sounds as numerous locks and dead bolts were undone. Finally, a smiling young man opened the door. "Dr. Booker! I can't believe it. It's so nice to see you. Come in."

Joseph Nori had been one of Abi's students. She knew him well. When he was nine years old, Joseph had moved with his parents from northern India. Nine years in India was long enough to acquire and retain a wonderful accent. Abi enjoyed listening to him, with his predictable highs and lows, like music in a loop. Even without the beautiful accent,

Joseph would have been her favorite student. He was brilliant, hardworking, and had an unusually good moral compass. Abi knew that she could trust him and that he would share in her excitement.

Abi looked back at the door as she entered the modest home. "Pretty impressive security."

"Yes. Two months ago I was robbed. Can you believe it? Just some feral youth I'm sure. However, they stole my laptop and my favorite Katy Perry poster."

"I am so sorry," said Abi. "Especially about your laptop."

"Yes. So I always lock my house now. Always. Even if I know someone is coming. Please forgive me. I'm just packing to leave. I'm flying to Malaysia tomorrow on a dig, my first one since graduation. Dr. Booker, are you coming too? Is that why you are here?"

"No, no. Sounds fun, but you know I've put that life behind me. No more field work for me. I did bring something for you to look at, though, if you have time."

"Absolutely. I suspected that you had something interesting. Bring it to my work table."

Abigail smiled to herself as she placed her bundle on a large green table. Abi guessed that nearly every piece of furniture in the home of the young paleontologist came from Goodwill, quite a contrast to the examination table and surgical quality LED lighting system that probably had cost him thousands of dollars. Joseph positioned the brilliant white overhead lamp. Abi unrolled the bundle, and Joseph immediately started his examination.

Without touching the fossil he made his initial observation. "I would say a femur, perhaps an allosaurus?"

"You are correct, Joseph. That's why you were one of my favorite students."

He smiled. "Tell me, where did this come from?"

"A bulldozer dug it up at Hobbs Point yesterday."

"Yesterday? What is it doing here?" said Joseph, visibly growing uncomfortable and tense. "It should be in a field jacket.

No, it should still be where you found it so we could study the taphonomy. You always taught me to study the fossil in reference to everything else in the dig. We need to study the matrix, the other bones, how it was lying, everything. Dr. Booker, please explain to me what this is doing here?"

"Once again, you are a first-rate paleontologist," Abi said. "But please, don't get upset. Go ahead, turn it over."

"Goodness, I'm not sure I want to touch it. This is highly irregular. Is this some sort of a test? Perhaps a post-graduation ethics pop quiz? I've already graduated! I have my diploma right there on the wall. It says Joseph Nori, Masters of Science: Paleontology. It is framed and everything. You can't have it." Joseph began to pace back and forth, looking nervously at the fossil.

"Joseph, take it easy. You're correct. This is highly irregular. I took it from the project site because I needed to protect it. Leaving the fossil was not an option."

"*Protect it?*" Joseph asked.

"Yes. Go ahead and turn the femur over."

Joseph rubbed his chin and looked again at the fossil. He slowly turned the fossil. His jaw nearly dropped to the top of the green table. Then, he grabbed a magnifying glass from the table in order to look more closely.

"Is this some sort of a prank?"

"No. No prank."

Joseph took a deep breath, rubbed his eyes, and looked again. "That is a spearhead."

"Yes, it is."

"There are indications of new bone growth, healing around the injury."

"Very good, Joseph."

Joseph looked at Abigail. "The allosaurus was alive when it was struck."

"Yes, it was," Abigail said.

Joseph dropped the magnifying glass and placed both hands on his face. "Do you know what this means?"

"Yes, I do," Abigail said.

"Goodness gracious. This . . . this is amazing. This is incredible. This . . . this should not be in my house."

"Believe me, Joseph, I'm as excited as you are," Abigail said. "We could really shock the scientific community with this one."

"We? What do you mean *we*? This is your discovery."

"Not so much. The fossil was just handed to me. I wanted to share this with someone who has the same passion for the truth and for science that I do. You and I are scientists. This is what makes us tick. New discoveries. New truths."

"Goodness gracious," said Joseph again, shaking his head in amazement.

"You said that. Look, I don't even know who to call anymore. We will need to present this in the right way. Actually, in a big way."

"A very big way," Joseph agreed. "How unfortunate that I need to leave tomorrow. You must not wait for me. A proper exhibition of this fossil to the proper establishment should be done soon."

"Yes," Abi said. "I suppose you are right. I'm just not as well connected anymore. No offense, but I certainly do not want to give this up to the local university."

"No, you are right. This requires nothing but the highest level of skill and expertise. I know a few places that could handle this. Let me sleep on it. If I think of just the right one, I will call you before I leave. Do you have a safe place to keep this for now?"

"Yes."

"Good," said Joseph. "But before you go, I need to look again and take measurements." Abi had trained Joseph well. Observations had to be made slowly and carefully. One could get into all sorts of trouble and head down an infinite array of crooked paths by jumping to conclusions. Or worse, by starting with some preexisting agenda, one could end up accepting only the data that agreed with a faulty premise.

Abi knew of many scientists who had fallen into that trap, especially when they were eager to have their name on a new discovery.

Joseph located a large caliper and held it against the fossil. "The femur measures eighty-nine centimeters. That means this guy was not quite fully grown. Here's the interesting part. Twenty-eight centimeters below the lesser trochanter is a ten-centimeter-long sharpened obsidian stone lodged . . . six centimeters into the shaft of the femur. Even with the per-mineralization process that formed this fossil, fracture callus and ossification is evident at the site of the spearhead. Remarkable."

Joseph reached for his camera.

"What are you doing?" Abigail asked.

"I must have a picture. A picture will help in case someone has some doubt. Remember other cases where human and dinosaur fossils were found together? For instance, the Texas 'Man Track' controversy?"

"I sure do," Abigail said. "A dry river bed had fossilized footprints of what appeared to be a human and a dinosaur walking during the same time period. But that was later disproven. The prints that looked human were actually metatarsal dinosaur tracks that had eroded. People were pretty worked up about that for a while. In that case and other similar cases, the scientific community has always managed to prove that they were fakes, forgeries, or misinterpretations."

"Clearly, this is no fake," Joseph said. "Nothing but the best for this fossil."

Abigail picked up the fossil. "You know, Joseph, this is a pretty big deal. Maybe you could postpone your trip?"

A huge grin spread across Joseph's face. "Yes, I know you are right. Under the circumstances I should. But you see, there is this girl named Sara that is also coming on the trip and . . ."

"Say no more, Joseph. I wish you both the best of luck."

"Yes, of course," said Joseph.

"How long have you known Sara?"

Joseph looked a bit uneasy. "Well, actually, I am not sure if she knows I exist. But that could all change. I mean, how could she resist?"

Abigail couldn't help but laugh. "Joseph, you are perfect. Now, I won't keep you any longer. One more thing: I wouldn't mention this to anyone else, even Sara."

∞ ∞ ∞ ∞ ∞ ∞ ∞

By the time Dr. Abigail Booker arrived home, night had fallen, and the house was dark. Fortunately, Ethan was still out with Gen. Abi had time to secure the bone in an ideal hiding spot in the broom closet. The entire back of the closet was a semi-loose section of sheet rock that was movable. Before she tucked the fossil away, Abi wrapped it tightly in burlap and secured it with duct tape. Then she placed the wrapped fossil deep inside the wall and pulled the sheet rock back into place.

Most likely, Ethan would soon forget all about the fossil, even though he had seen the weird black rock sticking out of the bone. Abi intentionally withheld the significance of the fossil from him. Abi wanted to keep it that way. She knew it was best to keep her son in the dark for now. This fossil held the potential to create a major disturbance. The less Ethan knew, the better. As long as the fossil was in the house, she would keep that information hidden from her son. Abi laughed to herself. A discovery that could change the scientific world was tucked into a spot where she and David used to hide Christmas presents from Ethan. Perhaps, she thought, this could be a gift to the world.

∞ ∞ ∞ ∞ ∞ ∞ ∞

"Shelly! You made it!"
Abi gave her sister a hug before sitting down on the bleachers. Shelly had never married and always felt she was

out of place and intruding whenever she visited Abi and David. Now, with David out of the house, the sisters were closer than ever. Shelly provided tremendous support when Abi needed her. Today they were both excited to watch Ethan play baseball. On a warm spring day, nothing was better.

The games were especially fun for Abi. She was treated like royalty since her son was having such a great season. Nearly everyone would smile at her, shake her hand, and tell her how great it was that Ethan was on the team. "We'd never be in first place without him." "Ethan makes all the difference in this team!" That sort of thing. She knew it was rather silly, but she loved every minute of it. Obviously she was extremely proud of her son, especially since the divorce had been so very difficult for him. The atmosphere of the ballfield did a marvelous job of taking her mind off the struggles of the past two years.

As usual, Ethan's childhood friend, Geneva, was in attendance. Abi often wondered if two children who grew up together could develop their relationship beyond a friendship. For Ethan's sake, Abi wished it would happen. Ethan would do well to end up with Gen. Abi had never known a more dedicated, intelligent young woman. Unfortunately, Gen was way smarter than Ethan. Abi laughed to herself. Gen was way smarter than anyone. Perhaps this would not be an issue. Without a doubt, Gen was very interested in her son. Hopefully, Ethan would notice.

"Gen's here again," Shelly said. "She certainly is a lovely young woman. Do you think Ethan has a clue?"

"Hard to know," Abi said. "They had a date last night, but Ethan tried to convince me it was nothing. They've been friends for so long he may not notice that she's all grown up. I do worry that Ethan might have difficulty committing to a more serious relationship . . . you know . . . because of David and me." Abi started to get a bit misty-eyed.

"OK, enough," Shelly said. "Ethan's up! Let's go, slugger!"

After two pitches, a chorus of boos began ringing out from the home crowd. *"Boo!"* yelled Abi, Shelly, and the rest of the home crowd as Ethan was intentionally walked with a man on second and third.

"The pitcher's just being smart. No way is he going to pitch to Ethan with ducks on the pond," said a man sitting next to Abi. "Let's just hope the next guy can drive 'em in."

"Question for you, Sis," said Shelly with a bit of a smile. "You know that I'm like twice the athlete that you are. How did Ethan get to be such a good ballplayer?"

"Twice?" exclaimed Abi. "What are you talking about? I remember racing you around the house when we were younger. We would go once around and I would nearly lap you."

"That's because you were thirteen, and I was four," Shelly said.

"Excuses, excuses," said Abi. She smiled. Having her sister there to talk to was wonderful.

"I know this is a shock, but David gets full credit for Ethan's athletic ability. They would spend hours together. Three years ago David's company was really struggling. He didn't have much work, so as a result, he was home a lot more. We were nearly broke, but thinking back on it, life was good. Ethan loved spending time with his dad. I'm sure David felt the same way. They would play catch for hours. David had time to build a batting cage in the backyard. Then the company took off, and the money started rolling in. Something inside of David changed. Suddenly he needed better machinery, better business partners, better employees, and better haircuts. Along with all that, he wanted someone younger and prettier to make his coffee. Who knew that stockbrokers knew how to make coffee?"

Shelly leaned toward Abi and held her hand.

Abi scanned the bleachers and the parking lot. "Anyway, with the Hobbs Point thing, he's back in town. I keep thinking maybe he'll come by to watch his son play."

"You're hoping that he will show up today, aren't you?"

Abi thought for a moment. "Well, maybe I am. Do you think that's crazy?"

"Off-the-chain crazy! You want to see him again—after what he did to you? I'm sure the nice men in their white suits would be happy to come and get you as soon as possible." Shelly paused. "At the same time, I understand. Really, I do. I know how happy you were together."

Abi smiled. She appreciated Shelly more than she could know. She was great therapy. Too soon, the game was coming to an end.

∞ ∞ ∞ ∞ ∞ ∞ ∞

Abi covered her eyes. "Aaugh! I hate this! Last inning and the score tied. Of course, Ethan is leading off."

"Stop whining, Sis, this is awesome. Come on, Ethan! We need a base runner!"

"You are such a jock. I wish we were either ahead by ten runs or behind," Abi said.

"OK, stop. Come on, stand up, and cheer for your son. Woo-hoo! Let's go, Eeeeth!!"

Ethan stepped to the plate. The unmistakable sound of a well-hit ball rang out as he lined the first pitch over the third baseman's head for a stand-up double.

The crowd rose, cheering wildly.

"You know," said Abi, "this will go straight to his already swollen head. Tomorrow I'm going to make him clean out our gutters."

"Shut up and enjoy the game," Shelly said. "Here comes the next batter. Let's go, Jimmy! Just a little hit! Here we go."

Jimmy Rose watched two pitches go by. Both of them were strikes. The third pitch was a nasty inside fast ball. He swung and weakly hit the ball off the handle, but the ball had just enough on it to clear the second baseman. Ethan waited long enough to make sure it wasn't caught, and then dug in his cleats and took off for home. The second baseman caught up with the ball just as Ethan was rounding third. The crowd rose to its feet as the second baseman wheeled and threw a strike to the catcher, who was blocking the plate. Ethan dove to the side, narrowly avoiding the catcher's foot planted in his path. He reached out with his left hand and brushed the plate with his fingertips.

"Safe! *Safe!!*" shouted the umpire, crossing his arms in big, wide movements to make the universal baseball sign for a safe slide at home.

Ethan rushed out to high-five Jimmy before the rest of the team engulfed them.

"Winning run! Two games straight!" shouted a man next to Abi.

"He gets it all from me," she replied with a laugh and a face beaming with pride.

Despite all the crowd noise and the numerous pats on the back, Abi suddenly realized her phone was ringing. "Hello. Hello?"

"Dr. Booker. This is Joseph. I—uh—need to . . ."

"Joseph? I can barely hear you. I'm at my son's ballgame, and he just scored the winning run! What did you say?"

"The fossil . . . again . . . my home."

"Joseph?" said Abi into her phone. "You want me to come back to your house now? I thought you were leaving. Joseph? There's too much noise. I really can't hear you."

". . . door unlocked."

"Unlocked?" asked Abi.

The call ended.

Abigail looked at her sister. "I have something I need to do. Would you do me a huge favor?"

"Of course."

"I told Ethan I would have a pizza ready for him after the game. The pizza is set to go and sitting in the refrigerator. Could you put it in the oven, and maybe wait for him?"

"What's up, Sis?" Shelly asked.

"I'm working with an old student of mine. He just called. I think I should see him."

Abi could tell that her sister was not completely buying the story. Fortunately, she did not press the point. "OK, I'll put the pizza in the oven. You take care."

Abigail caught Ethan's eye and waved at him before climbing down from the bleachers and heading for her car. She was glad to get out of the parking lot before everyone else. Joseph's voice had sounded odd, not the familiar, joyful singsong, but a voice that sounded stressed and jittery. *Why was Joseph upset? Could this have anything to do with the fossil?*

The twenty-minute drive to the edge of town seemed like an eternity. Abi was convinced that she hit every red light. Each time she stopped, her concern for Joseph grew. *He should be leaving on his trip, not asking to see me. What would possibly make him call?*

Abi jumped when her phone rang. She snatched it off the seat, expecting to hear Joseph's voice.

"Sis, I'm at your house. You were robbed."

"Shelly? What are you talking about?"

"When I got here, your front door was standing wide open. Looks like the crooks went through everything. Seems odd, though. Your laptop is still sitting on the kitchen table. Why didn't the crooks take that?"

Abi was now only a mile from Joseph's house. "Shelly, don't call the police. First I need you to do me a favor."

"Did you just tell me to *not* call the police? Abi, your house is a wreck. The thieves really tore it apart."

"Look, Shelly, I'll explain everything later. Right now, I need you to do something very important for me."

"I'm listening. I'm not liking it, but I'm listening."

"In the back of the broom closet there is a loose piece of sheet rock. Remove that and look behind that wall. Tell me what you find."

"You really are insane," Shelly said.

Abi turned onto the street in front of Joseph's house. "This is important, Sis."

"OK, but you will have some explaining to do later. I am here at your broom closet. The back doesn't seem to be loose. Ugh! The whole wall moved! Whoa! That is one awesome hiding place."

"What's in there?" Abi pleaded. Seconds moved slowly as Abi waited for Shelly to respond.

"A package of some sort, all wrapped up in duct tape."

Abi let out a huge sigh of relief.

"I don't suppose you'll tell me what it is?" Shelly asked.

"Later," Abi said. "For now, put that bundle back behind the wall. Then I suppose you should call the police. I'll be home soon."

"Finally, I have a sister that is interesting," Shelly said.

"I'll see you soon," Abi told her sister, then ended the call.

Abi immediately suspected that the thieves in her house were no ordinary robbers. She had been foolish. Abi had only been thinking of the scientific value of the fossil. But to the right buyer, on the black market, the dinosaur femur would be worth a lot. Abi had no idea exactly how much, but she assumed the value could be in the millions. Without a doubt, artifact thieves were after her fossil. This made sense. The theft of artifacts had surged recently. Thieves had targeted museums, auction houses, and heritage sites. Even archeological digs were being looted. Relics and artifacts were the new Holy Grail for thieves. It was all about the money. Big money. Abi had heard of a man in Nova Scotia who was recently arrested with relics worth more than ten million dollars. Ironically, one of the items in his possession was a rare edition of Darwin's *On the Origin of Species*. Abi shook her head in disbelief. *One day. That's all it took for the relic hunters to find my house. Did they find Joseph too?*

A number of cars were parked in front of Joseph's house. Abi had to parallel park a few doors down. She centered her car next to the curb and turned off the engine.

Things were happening too fast. She had to stop and think. She was glad to hear that the fossil was still safe. *But what about Joseph?* It was broad daylight and everything looked normal. *Shouldn't he be at the airport by now on his way to Malaysia with Sara? Something is wrong.* All of a sudden, Abi figured it out. *How could I be so stupid? Joseph gave me a signal—* " . . . door unlocked."

She picked up her phone to call him. As she held the phone in one hand, she restarted the car engine with the other.

After five rings Abi heard the answering machine message: "Hi, you have reached Joseph. If this is Sara, leave a message. Anyone else, I'm busy."

Joseph was in trouble; she was sure of it. What should she do? Calling the police was the only option that came to mind. As she reached for her phone again, she shrieked as it suddenly rang.

"Hello?" was all she could manage to say.

"Are you OK, Sis?" Shelly asked. "You sound kind of unnerved."

"Yes. Ahh, no. . . . Yes, I'm fine. It's ahh . . . the traffic. It's horrible."

"If you say so. I just got off the phone with the police. They are on their way to the house, but they want you to be here to provide them with a list of items that might be missing."

"I should be home in twenty to thirty minutes," Abi said.

Shelly paused. "Really? Even with horrible traffic?"

"Yeah, right," Abi said. "See you soon."

"You take care of yourself, Sis. I mean it," Shelly said.

As Abi hung up, she heard a car engine roar to life. In her rearview mirror a black sedan swerved sharply away from the curb. The car raced forward and slammed on its brakes inches away from her car, completely blocking her.

Abi reached the power door lock button just as two men sprinted up to her front passenger door. Pounding wildly on the window, one of the men shouted, "Come on out, Dr. Booker. We need to talk to you. Step out of the car. Now!"

Abi reached again for her phone. Her hands were shaking badly. She struggled to dial 911.

One of the men picked up a nearby landscaping rock, which he smashed violently against the passenger-side window. Tiny shards of safety glass exploded into the vehicle, covering the front seat and Abi. The other man lunged halfway through the broken window, attempting to open the door.

Abi pushed the gas pedal through the floor. Her car hurtled forward, smashing into the car in front of her, knocking it a few feet forward. The collision ejected the man hanging onto the car window. He flew backward out of the car and lay sprawled on the sidewalk. Abi was not thinking, just reacting out of fear for her life. Abruptly, she threw the car into reverse, colliding hard with the car behind her. Now she had room. She spun the wheel hard to the right and bounced up and over the concrete curb, nearly striking the two men trying to stop her. Abi swerved again to avoid a large elm tree and veered back onto the sidewalk. Only thirty feet ahead, she found a driveway and spun back onto the road.

Checking her mirror, she could see the two men running for their cars. One black sedan and one dark minivan quickly pulled onto the street. They were rapidly gaining ground. One man was on his phone.

Abi knew she could not outrun her pursuers. She also knew she could not stop. She began looking desperately for some busy public place to stop. Unfortunately, Joseph lived near the edge of town, and she was headed the wrong direction, out into the country. Abi could feel her pulse pounding behind her eyes. Her palms were sweating, and she tried to wipe them off one at a time on her jeans.

She grabbed her phone off the seat beside her. While keeping her eyes fixed on the road ahead, she attempted once more to dial 911. Before getting to the third digit, the dark sedan rammed her hard from behind. The phone flew out of her hand as she grabbed frantically for the steering wheel.

She glanced up at her rearview mirror. The menacing black sedan was inches behind her. The man behind the wheel was motioning wildly for her to pull to the side of the road.

"Not gonna happen," she murmured to herself, although she had no idea what to do. She couldn't just keep driving. With no buildings or other cars in sight, maybe she should stop and take her chances. Then again, that seemed like a really bad idea. She didn't know what they might have done to Joseph. And certainly she had no way to know what they would do to her. She couldn't help but feel sickened deep in the pit of her stomach. Evil and wickedness seemed to appear every time money was at stake.

Another crash! This time she was hit so hard she swerved off the road onto the shoulder. Abi overcorrected, sending her car all the way back across the road to the other lane. Somehow she regained control of the vehicle. She also had to control her thinking. Where were the other cars? People should be coming home from work. Other people would help her. Did Joseph live in such an isolated area that traffic was nonexistent?

She was a scientist and could always solve problems. With the phone far down in the foot well, she could not use it without stopping. Possibly she could stop quickly, grab the phone, and dial for help before they grabbed her. If she was not able to dial in time, that could be a mistake. Maybe she could just keep driving. She had to see another car eventually. But how much longer could she keep her car on the road? How fast was she going? Telephone poles were a blur as they flew by her shattered window. She glanced at her speedometer and was not surprised that it was pushing ninety. Perhaps she could just drive off the road, deep into the adjacent field. Then she could get out and make a run for it, possibly hide in the tall grass. No, they would be on her too soon.

She couldn't help wishing that David was here to help her. She also thought about Ethan. An hour ago, on a beautiful afternoon, she watched him score the winning run. How she wished she had never seen that bone. She could only think of one other thing to do. She said a prayer: "God protect me, and protect my son."

Abi's head snapped back. She nearly blacked out from the impact as she was rammed a third time, this time even harder. Abi fought with all her might to grab the wheel and stay focused. It was no use. Her car veered completely off the road, heading for a huge steel beam, which was the first of many beams holding up the bridge spanning the Rocky River. Abi spun the steering wheel wildly but still clipped the beam hard, launching her car violently onto the bridge deck. Even though pieces of her car were falling off everywhere, she still carried tremendous speed. The car spun in a complete circle before crashing through the railing high above the river. Her car flew into the air, twisting as it fell . . .

∞ ∞ ∞ ∞ ∞ ∞ ∞

*T*hree weeks later . . .
     Tall grass whipped against Ethan's legs as he emerged from the tree line above Hobbs Point carrying his favorite aluminum bat. A few strands of sweaty brown hair fell across his tear-streaked face. Ethan remembered the first day he had been here, but tonight was different. His mother was never coming back. Everything was his dad's fault. He picked up speed striding across the scarred landscape, moving closer to the bulldozer. His grip tightened on his bat. At seventeen years old, he was not too young to desire revenge. Tonight his father would pay a price for all he had done.

Ethan was now close enough to the huge machine that he could make out its brash yellow color by the starlight.

The massive silver blade, designed for ripping into the earth, sneered at the path before it. He grabbed the dozer's handle and swung easily up into the cab. The amount of electronics surrounding the operator's seat astounded him. Two huge joysticks extended toward him, each with elaborate diagrams for controlling the treads and the blade. Next to them were numerous displays—all black now. In front of him a large electronic monitor emitted a greenish light. He looked up into the giant windshield and saw his own eerie reflection. People were right when they said he looked just like his dad.

With only a slight pause—as if thinking about what he was going to do one final time—Ethan drew back his bat and swung as hard as he could in the confined space. The glass shattered, scattering his reflection into a million pieces. He swung again, this time smashing the green display. The next swing claimed the joysticks, bending one at ninety degrees and taking the other off its base. Out of the cab, he scrambled along the top of one huge tread. With one powerful swing, he sent the smokestack far into the dark night. He jumped back to the ground and fumbled to find, then successfully unlatch, the engine compartment. He swung relentlessly into its midsection. Metal crashed into metal. Pieces flew off into the darkness. Fluid oozed down its side, forming a black, lifeless puddle. He continued pounding on the yellow beast until his eyes stung with sweat, his hands burned, and his bat turned into a mangled club.

Exhausted, he fell to his knees in the damp, cool grass. The sound of breaking glass and bending metal was now replaced by a single cricket in the distance. Ethan listened intently for a moment, but heard no sirens, no car doors slamming, no people shouting. He looked up at the wounded beast and smiled. Maybe he couldn't destroy it, but he had been able to inflict serious wounds.

Content with what he'd accomplished, Ethan returned to his newly repaired bike parked in the trees. He stuck the bat straight down the back of his shirt and started out on the long ride home. A warm wind beat against him, a sign that spring was quickly giving way to summer. He couldn't understand why the sweat running down his arms was stinging his hands. The nicks and dents in his bat scraped against the skin on his back. By the time he climbed the stairs to his bedroom, his shoulders and arms were cramping, and his hands throbbed. He looked at his palms and grimaced. Four large blisters were the culprits causing this pain. Two had ripped open and were filled with blood and dirt. He was too tired to take a shower. Before collapsing on the bed, he picked up a framed photograph from his nightstand. A woman with brown curly hair stared back at him.

"Happy birthday, Mom," was all he said before gingerly setting it back down.

CHAPTER THREE

*Miracles are a retelling in small letters of the
very same story which is written across the whole
world in letters too large for some of us to see.*
— C. S. Lewis[2]

The morning sun shone brightly on Ethan's face. He blinked at the light, rubbing the sleep and a bit of grit out of his eyes. As he had done every day for the last three weeks, he looked at the picture of his mother on his nightstand. From this point on, that was the only way he would ever be able to see her. As he pushed himself to the edge of the bed, the stabbing pain in his hands suddenly reminded him of the previous night. No matter. He was still pleased with what he had done, happy that he was the one causing the pain for once.

After a quick shower he headed down the stairs. The smell of maple syrup was thick in the air, and he heard bacon sizzling as he neared the kitchen. He found his aunt standing in front of the stove with a flowered apron tied over a pair of shorts and tank top. She was nine years younger than his mom and a couple of inches taller, but Ethan found all the similarities—her hair, her mannerisms, her pattern of speech—a bit unnerving.

"Morning, Aunt Shelly," Ethan said. "Smells great, but I gotta go!"

"Hold on there, slugger! I made your favorite today, pancakes and bacon. You will sit down and eat!"

Ethan decided not to argue, especially with a spatula pointed menacingly in his direction. He kept his hands out of sight and made his way to the table, where a stack of eight pancakes towered on his plate.

"Got a phone call from your father early this morning," Shelly said. "Must have been some night last night."

"Last night?" asked Ethan hesitantly. "What happened?"

"Well, you know how his construction company is in charge up at Hobbs Point?"

"Of course," said Ethan. "Everyone talks about it. Now people are saying it's one of the biggest in Oregon." Ethan said the very words as though he were disgusted by the fact.

Shelly smiled. "So you *do* keep track of your father's accomplishments. I'm glad."

Ethan knew what Shelly was trying to do. His mother was gone, but he still had a dad. After the accident Shelly stepped right in, even though she too was grieving. Shelly was awesome helping out. But this was not her job. She was preparing Ethan to go and live with his dad. *No way will that ever happen.* For now, Ethan sidestepped that discussion. "I suppose Dad enjoys building all those million-dollar lots for those rich people. I heard that Mr. J. Sterner himself is building on one of those lots. I heard progress on his lot was delayed because of the dinosaur bones."

"That's true, but I have breaking news this morning," his aunt said. "Apparently, someone beat the tar out of one of your father's bulldozers last night. A bulldozer! Think of it! The police and your dad figure one those radical environmentalists must have been involved."

"Sounds like they have it all figured out. You know what? I think I'll head out there. Might be kinda fun to see what a beat-up bulldozer looks like." Ethan's aunt gave him a side-ways look.

Ethan grabbed his keys and headed for the front door. "Oh, and thanks for the cakes."

"Wait a minute," she said. "You seem rather pleased about this."

Ethan shrugged. "Shouldn't I?"

Shelly sighed. "Your father is a good man, Ethan."

Ethan did have some fond memories of his father—the camping trips in the Sierras, salmon fishing, and countless backyard baseball games. Ever since he was old enough to swing a bat, Ethan dreamed of being a major leaguer. His dad spent hours with him, patiently throwing pitch after pitch. When he did connect with the ball, his dad would cheer wildly as Ethan trotted around an imaginary base path, waving his cap to the imaginary fans. David would be waiting at home plate with a hug. Later, his father built him an entire batting cage. Ethan would stand at home plate, smacking ball after ball until his dad's arm was aching. Ethan loved it.

But that was before. One day his dad left. At first, his mom would say that Dad was working late. If it was morning and he wasn't around, his mom would say that Dad had to leave early for work. If she was crying, she had something in her eye. But the lying couldn't go on forever. The truth was painful. And the painful truth was that his dad had better things to do than to be his father. Sometimes believing the lies was easier.

"And . . ." Shelly said, pausing, "your dad would like to get together with you. I think it's a good idea."

"Not a chance."

"Ethan, there's no way I can possibly understand what you are going through. But a teenager needs a parent. He is your father."

"Mom and I were perfectly happy without him. If he hadn't come back, pushing that dinosaur bone at her, Mom would still be alive."

"It was an accident, Ethan. That's all."

Ethan's eyes welled up. He had told himself that he wouldn't cry anymore. "Like I said, Aunt Shelly, it's not going to happen. I don't want to see my dad ever again."

Ethan found it easier to focus on his anger for his father rather than the sorrow for his mother. Better to feel his hands throbbing in pain than to reach for her and feel nothing. At the funeral, his dad had come up to him sniveling about how sorry he was for everything. When he had tried to hug his son, Ethan had pushed him aside. People standing nearby were horrified, but that shove had helped Ethan make it through the day.

Ethan was anxious to drive up to Hobbs Point. He wondered how it would look in the daylight, if the bulldozer was trashed beyond repair and if work was halted for the day. He eagerly headed for the door. Before he got there, the doorbell rang.

Ethan was in no mood for company as he opened the door. But on the front step stood Gen. Geneva Marie Hartman was her full name. Her parents had traveled extensively throughout Europe, for business and pleasure. Early in their marriage, the Hartmans had found Geneva, Switzerland, to be the most beautiful, sophisticated, inspiring, peace-loving jewel on the face of the earth. The name fit her perfectly.

Gen was a great friend. Of course, Ethan knew that she was becoming more than that. The problem was that Geneva was amazing. She was the smartest person in school, and she already knew she wanted to become a molecular biologist. As tall as Ethan, she had long reddish-brown hair, a sprinkling of freckles, and spectacular blue eyes. In short, she was smart and hot. Ethan had no clue why she still hung around with him. The thing that most intrigued Ethan was her deep and unshakable sense of purpose. She knew without a doubt that she would someday change the world. She wasn't sure how, exactly, but she would be involved with something truly important. Ethan often wondered where that came from.

One thing was certain: Gen had what Ethan could only describe as an unshakable faith. She would often remind Ethan that God was in control. Of course, that seemed ridiculous now. If God was in control, why would his dad leave? And by the way, why did his mom drive off a bridge and plunge into a river? But Gen's faith was unflinching. Her resolve and her passion only helped to further convince him that Gen had moved way out of his league. Even so, they had been best friends forever. They knew everything about each other—their secrets, their ridiculous dreams, their fears. Everything.

Ethan tried his best to appear completely together. Apparently, he did not fool Gen. Without saying a word, she stepped inside and wrapped her arms around him. Ethan was amazed how comforting her hug felt. Her warmth and her hair falling on his neck offered far more encouragement than thinking about his aching hands all day.

"Thanks, Gen. I guess I needed that."

She hugged him again.

"Excuse me. Break it up. Underage children are present." Gen's little brother Raymond leaned his head inside the open door. "For Pete's sake, I'm only twelve. You'll give me a complex or something."

Ethan backed away from Gen and dried his eyes. He actually liked Raymond. For a kid, he was fun to have around. He was goofy-looking, in a preteen sort of way. His uncombed dark hair was sticking up at odd angles, his glasses were too big for his face, and his teeth were making some orthodontist very happy. Still, as beautiful as his sister was, Ethan assumed Raymond would soon grow into a handsome young man.

"My folks are out of town again, so I'm babysitting," Gen explained.

"Babysitting—there's a great expression," Raymond groaned. "Hey Ethan, how many popcorn balls do you want to buy?"

"Huh?" Ethan grunted.

Raymond was carrying a cardboard box. The top was open. Colorful red and green cellophane paper stuck out of the top. "I'm selling popcorn balls. We're raising money for our middle school debate team. Matching sport coats and ties don't grow on trees, you know."

"Not now," said Gen.

"I don't like popcorn balls," said Ethan.

"No one does," Raymond said, "but that's not the point, is it? They are two dollars each."

Gen grabbed her little brother by the shoulders and swung him backward out the door. "Sorry about that," she said. "We can't stay. I just wanted to see how you were doing."

"Thanks, Gen, but I'm fine. Actually, I was just heading up to the construction site. Want to go for a ride?"

"Sure," said Gen.

"Are we taking the Monte?" Raymond asked.

"Yep," Ethan answered.

"Let's roll," said the excited popcorn ball salesman, already halfway down the sidewalk.

They climbed into Ethan's '71 Monte Carlo. The classic muscle car had dark bronze paint, a black vinyl roof, dual exhausts, and plenty of chrome. Even though the car was old, Ethan loved the shape, and he kept it running like new. In four months he had completely rebuilt the engine. Not bad for a seventeen-year-old without a dad. Raymond pushed the seat forward and jumped into the back, rolling the window all the way down. Gen rode shotgun, sliding into the soft black leather bucket seat. Ethan turned on his favorite CD. He listened for a bit, changed his mind, and turned it down. He felt like talking.

"Back at the house, I said I was doing fine. Actually, I'm not sure about that."

"It's only been three weeks since the funeral, Ethan."

"That wasn't a funeral. I'm not sure what it was. No casket, no burial. Just a bunch of flowers sitting around a

five-year-old framed photo of Mom. Usually you at least get
to see a body and say good-bye." Ethan's cheeks turned red.
He bit his lower lip.

"Would you like me to drive?" Gen asked.

Ethan took a deep breath, ignoring her question. He
looked up at his rearview mirror, staring a bit too long.

"What is it, Ethan?"

"Nothing. Absolutely nothing. I just keep having this feeling that I'm being watched or followed. The school coun-
selor said I have a 'mild' case of paranoia. I guess this whole
thing has made me crazy."

"Everyone grieves in their own way, Ethan."

"I'm just not convinced that it's grief." Ethan checked his
mirror once again, and then turned up the music. He was
done talking.

A few minutes later, they arrived at the edge of the massive construction project west of town that the locals already
referred to as Snobs Point. Of course, no one Ethan knew
would be moving here, although he had certainly heard of
Mr. J. Sterner, the cable TV guy.

Everything was progressing nicely with the exception of
the north side. After the heavy equipment uncovered the dinosaur bones, work on that section was halted indefinitely.
For now, a tall, heavy-duty chain-link fence surrounded that
area. The fence was covered with a dark green tarp prevent-
ing anyone from seeing inside. In front of the fence was a
trailer, complete with a satellite dish on the top. Ethan had no
idea that dinosaur bones needed so much protection.

"What's going on over there?" Gen asked. She pointed to
the west end, which was buzzing with activity. A large number of people seemed to be clumped together.

"They're probably looking at the bulldozer."

"What's so interesting about a bulldozer?"

Ethan smiled and rolled the Monte forward. Driving
through the construction site was easy today since it was
practically deserted. Yellow and green machinery sat idle,

temporarily abandoned. The west end, however, was littered with people. Workers in blue coveralls and orange hard hats were milling about even though no work was being done. Other locals came to gawk, and the police were everywhere. Yellow crime tape sectioned off a large area around the bulldozer. As the car moved closer, Ethan was already disappointed. Broken glass covered the ground, and some of the dents were impressive, but in reality the huge machine didn't look all that bad. Last night Ethan felt so powerful. He felt like he was committing the ultimate act of defiance, delivering a definitive statement. Now he realized he was just a pathetic juvenile delinquent, vandalizing property. On the bright side, no one was working today. That by itself would cause some amount of grief for his dad.

Ethan, Gen, and Raymond got out of the car to get a better look at the bulldozer. Nearby, a small group of irritated construction workers were talking to the police. They kicked at the dirt with their boots, creating small clouds of dust, as they offered short unhelpful comments. Ethan was able to catch small snatches of the conversations going on.

"The machine was like this when we got here . . . didn't see anyone . . . nothing suspicious . . ."

". . . no prior threats? . . . no clue who mighta done it?"

Raymond leaned against the yellow tape to get a closer look.

"Hey, kid, stay away from there," a policeman warned.

Raymond nodded to the officer and moved away. He and Ethan followed Gen, who had moved to eavesdrop on another group of workers.

". . . no-good environmentalist nut-jobs. Unemployed freaks."

". . . no overtime paycheck this week!"

Ethan felt uncomfortable. No one could possibly suspect him. Still, he had the unnerving sensation that everyone was looking at him. He started to sweat. He jammed his red hands into his pockets and turned away.

"Geneva. Raymond. Let's go," he said.

As they headed back to the car, Gen looked at Ethan, "How did you know about this?"

"Dad called Aunt Shelly this morning. He told her all about it."

"Did you talk to him?"

"Are you kidding?"

"Well, I think it's just crazy."

"I thought it was totally cool," said Raymond.

"Who in their right mind would try to wreck a bulldozer?" said Gen.

"Those environmentalists didn't do anything. That's for sure," said Raymond.

"How do you know that?" asked Ethan.

"Did you see the size of those dents? No way some tofu-eating, sprout-loving greenie could cause that much damage."

Ethan couldn't help smiling at Raymond's assessment. "Maybe the person that did it had a good reason."

"A good reason?" said Gen. "Sure, a delusional thug might reason that it was completely logical to mutilate a bulldozer."

Ethan glared at her.

"Fine," she said. "This isn't a good time to argue with you."

Gen changed the subject, "Do you want to go up to the north end and look at the dinosaur dig? We might be able to see something."

Ethan shook his head, "That's out of the question."

"Maybe we can," said Raymond. "We might be able to peek through a crack. You never know. We might be able to see a huge bone or something."

Ethan kicked at the dirt. "I'm not going anywhere near that area. That hole in the ground has a lot to do with what happened to my mom."

"You're overthinking this," Gen said. "Your mom died in a car accident. She wasn't anywhere near here when . . ."

Ethan looked at her. He knew the rest of the sentence all too well. He finished Gen's sentence for her. ". . . When her car plunged off the bridge, landing on its roof in Rocky River."

"Of course, she was interested in the dig," Gen said. "After all, how often does a paleontologist get a dinosaur in her backyard? That's why your dad had called her."

"There was more going on than just a few bones," said Ethan. "She was really worked up about something. I don't mean excited. More like agitated, you know, wound up. Something big was up, or she wouldn't have acted that way. I'm convinced that whatever it was had something to do with her accident. Sure, the television station called it an accident. Investigative reporters and cameras were all over that bridge. They should have found something. No way was that an accident."

Ethan was hyperventilating. Gen put her hand on his arm. "My fault. I shouldn't have brought it up. We do need to remember that God is in control. Everything will be all right."

They all climbed into the Monte. Ethan turned the ignition and checked his rearview mirror. "Yeah, right," he muttered.

They were quiet as they drove. As they approached town, Gen had an idea. "I have a couple of chores to do back home. When I finish, how about I come back to your house? I'll bring a couple of movies."

"No chick flicks," said Raymond.

"Agreed," said Ethan.

Ethan pulled into Gen's driveway. "That's right. Your parents are out of town. Maybe I should come to your house instead."

They both looked back at Raymond.

"What'd I do?" he said.

Gen smiled. "I'm glad to see you're feeling better. But your house will work just fine for all of us. I'm sure your Aunt Shelly will enjoy watching movies too."

Gen gave Ethan another hug. Maybe she was out of his league. But for right now, Ethan was just glad she was here when he really needed a friend.

"I mean what I said, Ethan. What happened to your mom was terrible, and I know you miss her a lot, but your mom died in an accident. An accident, Ethan. Try to let it go."

Gen and Raymond jumped out of the car. Ethan drove home, proceeded straight to his room, and refused to let anything go. There had to be some connection between his father, the dinosaur bone, and his mother driving off a bridge. He knew it.

No, he wouldn't let it go. But this time, he didn't cry.

CHAPTER FOUR

I was a young man with uninformed ideas.
I threw out queries, suggestions, wondering
all the time over everything; and to my
astonishment the ideas took like wildfire.
People made a religion of them.

—Charles Darwin[3]

The garage had become a sanctuary for Ethan. He kept it spotless and perfectly organized. He had control here. His tools were all arranged neatly on a large white pegboard that covered the entire front of the garage. Ethan knew the location of every tool, and he knew how to use each one. He knew how to take his car apart and put it back together. Everything here made sense. Everything had order.

He pulled the Monte into the garage and raised the hood. He decided to give it a tune-up, even though it was running perfectly. Sometimes he could think more clearly while he was working with his hands. He grabbed a spark plug wrench from its home on the pegboard and got to work.

"Hey, Slugger."

Ethan peered around the hood. He could see his father leaning against the driver's side door.

"Saw you and Gen up at the construction site this morning. I always knew that you two would become an item one of these days."

"An item?" Ethan sneered. "Is that what you used to call it?"

"She's a nice girl. I was just wondering if it was anything serious."

"I guess you'll just have to spy on us some more to find out."

"Look, Son, we haven't had a decent conversation for quite some time."

"And we're not having one now," said Ethan. "By the way, whose fault do you think that is?"

"I understand how you must feel. You have every right to be angry at me for leaving."

"Leaving was fine. I'm angry that you came back."

"That's not fair, Ethan. You can't blame me for what happened to your mom. I never thought that . . ."

"Right again," Ethan said. "You never thought."

"Listen to me. Yes, I did call your mother about the bones that my crew uncovered. I called her because I knew she would be interested. I thought I was doing her a favor. Sure, I'll admit I had been looking for an excuse to call, to hear her voice. This was a really good excuse. After you walk out on someone, you need one," he said. Even Ethan could sense the real hurt in his dad's voice.

Ethan continued to work under the hood. "Can't tell you how glad I am that you called her? Things have been just great ever since."

David paused for a moment, attempting to regroup. "I was wondering, you know before the accident, did she say anything to you about . . . the dinosaur bone?"

"What?"

"You know . . . the bone. The fossil that I gave to her that night in the trailer. I was just wondering what might have happened to it. Have you seen it around?"

"Nope."

"She didn't talk about it or tell you where it might be?"

"No, Dad. Seriously, how could it possibly matter?"

"Just curious. You see . . ."

Ethan's dad abruptly stopped his line of questioning. Ethan was not about to give him any information. David changed course.

"Tell you what. I haven't been completely out of touch, you know. I read in the papers that you led the league in homers this year. Not bad for your first year on varsity."

Ethan said nothing, but turned away, looking for another tool.

"What do you say we go out back to the batting cage? I could pitch you some balls. I'd love to see that swing of yours." Ethan's dad started to look around for the baseball equipment. "I seem to remember we kept the baseball stuff in this corner."

Ethan cringed as he looked back at his father. David spotted Ethan's bat and pulled it out of the corner.

His father stared at it. Flecks of bright yellow paint covered the mangled barrel. All the color drained from his dad's face. The bat dropped to his side as if it suddenly had grown very heavy.

Ethan slammed the hood of his car shut and stared directly at his father. "What are you going to do, Dad? Take me to the police?"

His father appeared to be in shock. Eventually, he managed to speak. "You . . . did a lot of damage."

Ethan knew he didn't need to reply. For once, his father understood him perfectly.

He looked at Ethan once more and walked out of the garage. He stopped before he got in his car. His hands seemed to be shaking, and he struggled to find his voice. "I . . . I lost her too, you know."

He drove away in his silver Buick. The anger in Ethan's gut was still very real as his father disappeared around the corner. For the first time, though, he felt something *new*. Along with his anger, he also felt a twinge of regret. Ethan carried his mangled bat to the garbage can and tossed it in. His mom had only been gone for three weeks, but now it felt like forever. He stared at his own car and realized that, along with the anger and the regret, suddenly he felt very much alone.

Ethan jumped when his cell phone rang. No number was displayed, just an out-of-area message. He answered it anyway.

"Who is this?"

"Ethan, it's your mom."

The cell phone slipped from his hand. He watched it fall to the floor as if in a dream. The phone bounced along the garage floor, as if in slow motion, coming to rest under his car. Ethan slowly bent down, confused why his phone was on the floor. Nothing made sense. The room began to spin. He sat down so he wouldn't fall down.

"Ethan, talk to me. Ethan!"

The voice was familiar, although oddly distorted coming from the phone upside down on the floor. Strange, the voice almost sounded like his mother. Somehow he slid himself closer and forced himself to pick up his cell phone. He stared at the cracked screen and wondered why it still worked.

He swallowed. Hard. ". . . Mom?"

"Ethan, listen to me. I know this doesn't make sense, but please don't hang up."

This wasn't a dream. Ethan struggled to focus. He managed to clear his dry throat. "Mom . . . I . . . what happened to you?"

"I can't explain now," she said. "But I need your help."

All he could do was hold on to the phone. Even though he was already on the floor, he still felt as though he might pass out.

"Ethan! Stay with me!"

"I'm here. Talk to me, Mom."

"A very important item," continued Ethan's mom, "is hidden in our house. I need you to bring it to me."

". . . important item," Ethan repeated. He was still in a haze. His brain was working so hard trying to understand how he could possibly be talking to his mother through a broken phone. Focusing on her simple directions was difficult.

"That's right. I need you to bring it to me."

"Where is it?" Ethan asked.

"In the broom closet behind the bottom shelf is a loose section of sheet rock."

Ethan was gradually regaining control of his thoughts. This was real. His mother was alive, and he was talking to her. ". . . The back of the broom closet? You mean where you used to hide my Christmas presents?"

She chuckled slightly. "Yes, where we hid your presents. I also need clothes and some cash. Do you know where I keep the emergency cash?"

"Yes. How about credit cards?"

"No, just the cash and clothes."

"What's going on, Mom? Please tell me what's going on."

She left a long pause. "I think someone was trying to kill me, Ethan. They might still be."

"Who? Why would they do that?"

Another long pause.

"Mom?"

She whispered, "It is possible that they are still listening. I have to go. I'll call you back later. I love you, Ethan."

The call ended.

"I love you, too," Ethan said, still in a daze. The phone fell back to the floor. His head spun as he slumped back against the bumper. She was alive. His mom was alive, but she was in trouble. He tried desperately to remember what she said. Her instructions. His mother had given him specific instructions. Someone had tried to kill her. She needed an important item. She was alive.

Ethan closed his eyes and attempted to control his breathing. His heart pounded and he realized he was covered in sweat. Suddenly he realized he wasn't alone. Gen and Raymond were standing next to his car looking down at him. Gen's arms were full of movies. Her face looked troubled and pale.

Ethan tried hard to smile at her. "First, I have paranoia. Now I have a whole new phobia. I'm talking to dead people."

"That's not a phobia," said Raymond. "I think you have more of a neurosis."

Gen dropped her movies and squatted down next to him.

"What's going on, Ethan?"

∞ ∞ ∞ ∞ ∞ ∞ ∞

*I*n a motel room across town . . .
　"Hey, Boss. Wake up. We got her."

A man with a blond crew cut heard the words he had been waiting for and sat up on the edge of the bed. He looked around the room, glad that he would not be staying much longer. Pizza boxes towered high in one corner. Newspapers and magazines covered the only table in the room. One small window did little to lessen the stench of stale beer and old socks.

He cleared his throat. "Good work, Broderick," he said in an odd, icy whisper.

The other man in the room wore headphones that were plugged into a black electronic board with numerous LED lights and digital displays. Next to him was a cheap flatscreen television tuned to a soccer game. "You were right, Mr. Frost. I would have bet a thousand dollars that the fossil lady was dead for sure. But I got her clear as a bell, talking to that son of hers."

For three weeks, the three-man surveillance team monitored every phone call to Ethan, Dr. Booker's sister, her ex-husband, and a young paleontologist named Joseph. Mobile surveillance had also been deployed to monitor Ethan's movements. They found him to be a seventeen-year-old boy with no known history of terrorism, although he had recently demonstrated violence toward a bulldozer. The bulldozer incident had been observed by a member of a different team stationed at the site of the fossil discovery. The son of Dr. Booker was determined to be the only target that might prove beneficial in the recovery of the asset. Frost knew from observing Ethan's body language that the target sensed he was being watched.

Despite the appearance of the room, the operation was extremely well organized. Frost demanded a tight and professional operation. Modern techniques of surveillance and asset recovery were highly effective. Tactics had been developed by military intelligence from a variety of approved sources. Surveillance had evolved into a science incorporating human behavioral studies, calculated outcomes, and appropriate use of force. The men running the operations were always ex-military and usually ex-CIA. This high level of surveillance was only implemented when the value of the asset was enormous.

Frost cleared his throat. "Broderick, what did she say?"

"She told her kid to bring her the fossil. Hard to believe, but it's still in the house. I don't know how it could be—we tore that place apart."

Frost cleared his throat. "So—do you know where she is?"

"Negative. She didn't say, and I couldn't get a fix on her location. But she told her son that she would call again. She's no dummy. The doctor lady even told her kid that someone might just be listening. Can you believe it?"

Frost would believe anything. In his twenty-five years as an expert in the field he had seen it all. He had been shot at many times, run over twice, and attacked by a Komodo dragon. On one particularly dangerous operation, he was ambushed and stabbed in the throat. Fortunately the blade missed his carotid, but partially severed his vocal cords. The injury left him with an icy whisper of a voice, but in spite of his age and injuries, he was better at his job now than ever. Unfortunately, this simple job had become a lengthy one. The asset should have been easily located in Dr. Booker's house long ago. It was not. Also unfortunate was Dr. Booker's decision to not bring the asset into Joseph's house after he was encouraged to call her. Of course she would have found herself tied up next to Joseph for a while, but the asset would have been retrieved, and their troubles would have soon been over.

For Dr. Booker, her troubles were just beginning. Actually, Frost was pleased that she was alive. There was no need for her to drown in the Rocky River. Besides, she was apparently the only person who knew the location of the fossil. All Frost had to do was wait for her to resurface—literally, after her plunge into that river—three weeks later.

Frost was a veteran. He knew that many factors contribute to the phenomenon of a person in hiding eventually turning up. One is that the missing person may have felt threatened, and, for some reason, three weeks seems like sufficient time for the threat to go away. At the same time, the person has missed family and friends. They have a strong need to hear a familiar voice. The person in hiding has entered this delicate balancing act: they need enough time to have elapsed in order to feel safe, while at the same time, there is a powerful desire to contact loved ones. The balancing act always lands on three weeks—give or take a couple of days. Frost was well aware that people were much like mindless, submissive sheep. This made his job so much easier.

"Soon we can go home, Rickie. Time for a well-deserved paycheck. All we have to do is monitor the home with mobile surveillance. As soon as the kid exits his home with the asset, our job is done."

"Why don't we just go and get it now?"

"Dr. Booker's son has got the fossil. I would not underestimate this young guy. I got a feeling he will not scare easily. Better to wait and watch. He'll go to his mother soon. For now, get those headphones back on and let me know if you get any more conversations in the next twelve hours. After that, sweep this room completely and get us checked out."

Frost cleared his throat and left the room.

CHAPTER FIVE

——————➤

Man will occasionally stumble over the truth, but usually manages to pick himself up, walk over or around it, and carry on.

— Winston Churchill[4]

"Can you see anything?"

"Give me a second," said Ethan. He was lying on the floor with his head inside the broom closet. He had pulled the loose section of sheet rock out and set it next to him. Behind the panel was a small space between the wall studs. Ethan reached in and pulled out a bundle. Roughly the size of a baseball bat, the package was bound in brown burlap completely wrapped with duct tape.

"Is that a dinosaur bone?" Raymond asked.

"It must be," said Ethan. "I'm glad it's still here. After the accident, the house was crawling with investigators. They said they were looking for evidence. I'm guessing this is really what they were looking for."

Ethan, Gen, and Raymond stood staring at the bundle in Ethan's hands. This inanimate lump had already taken on a life of its own. Ethan half expected the thing to stand up and start walking around. Surprisingly, he did not feel an outburst of anger toward the bone. After all, this was the source of all the trouble. Ethan could have easily passed the blame to the thing, this object. However, he knew that it is people who cause trouble—not things.

"Should we open it up?" Raymond asked.

"No, not now," Ethan said.

"Who would believe that this is causing so much trouble for your mom?" Gen asked.

"So why don't we call the police?" Raymond wondered.

"She isn't safe," Ethan said. "Whoever tried to kill her might try again if they knew she was still alive. She's better off if no one knows. None of us may be safe. Something weird is going on. You two shouldn't get involved."

"Too late," Gen said.

"That's for sure," Raymond said. "This is just getting interesting."

Ethan knew not to insist. Besides, they were already involved. "OK, that bundle will fit nicely in my green baseball equipment bag. My bag is big enough to carry two bats and lots of other gear. We need to throw in some of her clothes, too. Jeans, sweatshirt, T-shirt . . . umm, I suppose she'll need, you know, other stuff."

"Tell you what. Why don't you let me pack the other stuff?" Gen said, making clear she'd handle that aspect. "You get the cash. By the way, where's your Aunt Shelly?"

"Grocery store. She was going to get some snacks for movie night."

"Snacks?" said Raymond. "We've got popcorn balls."

Ethan ignored him and retrieved the emergency cash. Seven hundred twenty dollars was tucked into a plastic container in the back of the linen closet. This was not a great hiding spot, and Ethan wondered why the thieves that broke in weeks ago did not find it. He shrugged and grabbed all the cash. He went back to his mom's bedroom, where Gen was sitting on the edge of the bed, busy packing. When he got to the doorway, he stopped. In the midst of all the chaos, he was once again struck by the fact that his childhood pal, his best buddy, had become a beautiful young woman.

"Gen?"

Gen looked up from her packing. She pushed her hair out of her eyes and smiled at him. "What is it?"

"Am I still your best friend?"

Gen got up and moved toward Ethan. She took his hands in hers.

"Do you remember our very first day of school? We were six. I was wearing a yellow dress."

"I was wearing my favorite baseball shirt," said Ethan. "Mom has a picture of us somewhere."

"We were so excited that we held hands and decided to skip all the way to school. We were almost there when I tripped and fell on the sidewalk. You bent down and looked at my skinned knee. 'I'll kiss it,' you said, 'and make it better.'"

Gen stopped her story. She leaned in close to Ethan and gently kissed him on the cheek. "Yeah, you're still my best friend."

"Oh, *puhh-lease*," Raymond moaned. "I am definitely going to need serious therapy, and you two are going to pay for it."

Ethan laughed for the first time in weeks as they carried their items downstairs. Suddenly his cell phone rang.

It was Mom.

"Sorry I had to hang up before."

"Are you safe?" Ethan said.

"Yes."

"I've got your clothes and the money. Where are you?"

There was a pause before she answered. "We have to be careful. It is possible that they are listening."

"What are you talking about, Mom?"

"Just listen, Ethan. You can meet me for s'mores."

"S'mores? Mom, I don't understand."

"I can't imagine how hard it must have been for you these last three weeks, but I had to wait. I couldn't put you in danger. By now they must have given up, but there is no way to know for sure. Meet me for s'mores."

Ethan closed his eyes, forcing his brain to bypass the countless questions and focus on the meaning of his mother's message. Finally he understood. He remembered picnics with his mom and dad at a quiet, out-of-the-way place called Seaside Park. There was a wide sandy beach where they hunted for shells and starfish. At night Ethan would help his dad build a fire where they would roast marshmallows to make s'mores. They always stayed in a small motel near the beach.

"I know the spot," said Ethan.

"Good. I'm sorry to be so cautious. It may not be necessary. By now they must think I'm really dead."

"They? Who's *they*, Mom?"

"Just be careful, Ethan. They may be watching and try to follow you."

Then she hung up. Ethan stared at the phone in disbelief.

"She's talking in code, and said they might try to follow us. This is not going to do my paranoia any good at all."

"I'll check the street," Raymond said. He moved to the front window and peered out. "Hey, Ethan, you know how paranoia is all in your head? Well, I've got good news. You're not paranoid at all. You really *are* being watched."

Ethan and Gen crowded up to the window. Parked a few houses away was a minivan with dark tinted windows.

"Have you ever seen that car around here?" said Gen.

"No, never," said Ethan.

"You can tell it's a spy van," Raymond said. "They try to blend in by using a late model minivan. But those tinted windows are too dark to be street legal. Plus, that major antenna sticking out the roof really gives them away."

"How do you know that stuff?" asked Ethan.

"I read it in a book. You should try it sometime," he said.

"It makes sense," said Gen. "They can't find your mom. Since her body was never recovered, they're not entirely convinced that she's dead. You're their last hope, Ethan. They're hoping you will lead them right to her."

"I almost did," said Ethan, horrified at the thought. "Well, if anyone has a brilliant idea, now is the time."

"I do," said Raymond. He grabbed his box of popcorn balls and headed for the back door.

"What are you doing?" said Ethan.

"I'm still a long way from my sport coat and tie. Gotta sell these," he said, suddenly holding up the popcorn balls. Raymond dashed out the back door and ran around to the neighbor's. Ethan and Gen watched through the open side window as he smoothed his hair and rang the doorbell.

"Good afternoon," said Raymond. "I'm taking orders for delicious individually wrapped popcorn balls. How many would you like?"

"Is he out of his mind?" Ethan asked.

"Yes, but let's watch anyway," Gen answered.

Raymond repeated this at the next house before he crossed the street. After visiting two more houses, he walked right up to the parked minivan. Ethan and Gen leaned close to the open window, straining to hear. Gen grabbed Ethan's hand. As confident as Gen was, Ethan knew she felt scared for Raymond. She was supposed to be watching him, keeping him safe. Now she was letting him walk right up to a minivan filled with bad guys.

Raymond rapped on the tinted driver's window. He had to knock again before the dark window slid down a couple of inches.

"Whad'ya want, kid?"

Ethan and Gen could hear the irritated voice from the van. The man had an unusual voice, very hoarse and breathy, almost like ice. Although only a whisper, the voice was obviously loud enough to be heard by them. Raymond held the box right up to the car window.

The man cleared his voice. "Get lost, kid!"

"This is a really bad idea," said Ethan, heading for the door.

Gen grabbed his arm. "I don't like it either. But we have to wait."

The man in the car shouted again, "Like I said, get lost!"

Suddenly Raymond turned around, and in a voice loud enough for the whole neighborhood to hear, all but yelled, "You want to give me drugs? You want me to get in your car?"

"Shut up you little . . ."

"Someone call 911! This stranger wants to give me drugs!"

The tires of the van smoked and squealed loudly. Raymond stepped back and watched as the dark minivan accelerated down the block and out of sight. Raymond nonchalantly walked back to Ethan's house.

"You are unbelievable," Ethan said.

"Oh, I don't know," Raymond said. "I only sold four popcorn balls."

"We're in the clear," Gen said. "Put the bundle on top of everything in the sport bag. Let's go."

Ethan's cell phone rang. The out-of-area message appeared once again.

Ethan didn't wait to hear his mom's voice, but just started talking. "Mom, we're just leaving," he said as he reached for her bag of clothes.

After a long pause, Ethan heard the same odd voice that had come from the open car window only minutes before. "Interesting. I thought your mum was dead, Ethan."

Gen and Raymond were close enough to also hear the icy voice. Like Ethan, they stopped in their tracks.

"I'm glad she's alive." He paused to clear his throat. "Truly, I am. No need for anyone to die."

Gen looked out the front window as she heard a car screech to a stop. This time, the dark minivan pulled up directly in front of Ethan's house. Two men jumped out of the car. The one from the driver's seat was still holding a cell phone to his ear. He wore a dark gray sport coat with a black tie. He had a short blond crew cut, looked to be about fifty, and seemed to be in excellent shape. The other man also wore a dark gray sport coat but had on a blue T-shirt. He was approximately the same age, but not as fit. They moved quickly toward the house.

"Raymond! Lock the back door!" Gen shouted.

"Don't bother with the doors," the hoarse voice said. "We just need to talk."

"I'm calling the police," said Ethan.

"Please do. They would be fascinated to hear all about your mother. Be sure to tell them that she's still alive. They would love to know where she's hiding. That would save us all a lot of time."

Gen locked the front door just as the man on the phone reached it. His loud knock caused her to shriek.

"Really, no one needs to be afraid," the man with the icy voice said, still communicating with Ethan over the phone. "This is a simple matter. Give us the item, and we will leave."

"I don't know what you're talking about," said Ethan.

"Ethan, I'm tired of waiting. Three weeks is a long time to sit in your crummy hotel in your boring little town. Besides, I am more than a bit irritated by your little friend's antics. Waiting is over."

The other man was now pounding on the back door. He shouted around to the front, "It's locked, Boss!"

"Get upstairs," Ethan whispered to Gen and Raymond. Gen grabbed her brother's hand and started toward the stairs.

"Your mother told you where the package was hidden. Apparently the hiding spot was so good that it eluded my best men. But now you have it, and you will give it to me."

With a crash, both doors were kicked open.

"Ethan!" screamed Gen from the stairway.

The men converged on Ethan, but he was quicker. He grabbed the bag, the wrapped bone inside, and bolted up the stairs right behind Gen and Raymond.

"Quick!" he shouted. "My room!" Ethan shut and locked his bedroom door. He leaned hard against it but was nearly knocked back when someone rammed into it from the other side. The door held for now. Ethan motioned to his dresser. He left the door for a moment. Together with Gen, they slid the heavy dresser in front of the door and leaned against it just in time. With a loud bang, the door frame cracked, sending splinters into the room, but the dresser held.

"We're just wasting time," the man hollered.

Ethan continued to press hard against the dresser. He turned and whispered in Gen's direction. "Gen, in my closet is a trap door that leads to the attic. Go!"

She did not hesitate. Grabbing Raymond's hand they disappeared into the closet.

"Ethan!" the man shouted. "I hate to say this, but I'm getting a little angry."

Another loud crash. The door would not hold much longer.

Ethan flew to the closet. Gen was already pulling Raymond up through the trap door by his arms. Ethan was right behind. He pulled himself up just as his bedroom door completely gave way, sending the dresser crashing to the floor.

The man cursed loudly.

A warped, narrow board with yellow insulation on either side ran the length of the attic. At the far end was a small window.

"Where are you?" shouted the man. "Don't tell me you're hiding under the bed."

Gen was in the lead, crawling unsteadily along the narrow board toward the window. The board had never been nailed down. Now it rocked precariously as they scrambled across. All three coughed and squinted from the stirred-up dust and fiberglass. When they reached the other end, Ethan reached past Gen to open the window.

A massive oak tree stood in Ethan's backyard. A thick branch reached close to the attic window before angling away. The branch was swaying, moving in and out in the wind. Large oak leaves beat loudly against each other.

"You first, Gen." From the window to the middle of the branch was only two feet, but the branch was twenty feet in the air.

"Don't worry," Ethan said with as much assurance as he could muster. "I do this all the time when I sneak out of the house."

Gen put the straps of the sport bag through her right arm and over her shoulder. Timing the movement of the branch, she lunged out the window and aimed her foot directly for the center of the branch. Suddenly, the sport bag snagged on a loose shutter, jerking Gen sideways. Dangling twenty feet above the ground, she clung desperately to the bag. She tried to swing her foot out to catch the branch.

"Found 'em!" shouted the second man, who had now made his way into the room after discovering the trap door.

Ethan clutched both of Gen's arms just before the bag slipped from her grip. His hands were sweaty, but he quickly swung her to the branch.

"She made it. Raymond, go!" Raymond leaped out the window and made it easily to the branch. He immediately started following his sister through the leafy branches, down the big tree to the ground.

Both men were now on the narrow board, crawling quickly toward Ethan.

"Impressive effort, young man. You nearly escaped," the man with the icy voice said, at once with steadying himself on the board after nearly toppling. He was clearly a "professional," and used to risky situations like this.

Ethan turned his body sideways, leaning hard against a truss. With all his strength, he kicked the loose board with both feet. The board shifted violently, causing both pursuers to lose their balance. Their weight was more than enough to break through the attic ceiling, dropping them eight feet to the floor below. Loud crashing, with louder cursing, echoed from inside the bedroom. A plume of dust and insulation filled the attic.

"Gen, catch!" said Ethan as he leaned out the window in order to breathe. He unhooked the green bag from the shutter and tossed it to the ground. Gen caught it neatly. In only seconds Ethan scrambled down the tree.

"What happened in there?" Gen asked.

"Never mind. Quick, through the alley!"

Ethan, Gen, and Raymond sprinted away from the house, down the narrow alley.

"What are we going to do?" Gen said, starting to breathe hard, bent over, hands on knees.

"No clue," Ethan said.

Just as they reached the main road, a yellow van slammed on its brakes and pulled to stop in front of them. Ethan's aunt had come to their rescue. "Jump in!" she said.

They dove into the van. She sped off before they could even shut the doors.

"Everyone OK?" she asked, never taking her eyes from the road.

"Yeah," Ethan said. He had a million questions, but didn't know where to start.

"So," Raymond said, still breathing hard. "I suppose this means no movie night?"

CHAPTER SIX

Look at the behemoth, which I made along with you and which feeds on grass like an ox. What strength he has in his loins, what power in the muscles of his belly! His tail sways like a cedar . . .
—Job 40:15-17 (New International Version)

The yellow van moved steadily along the highway. Ethan, Gen, and Raymond were still dazed but starting to breathe easier. Looking out the window, Ethan could tell they were headed in the direction of Seaside Park.

Ethan leaned toward the front seat. "You've known all along."

"Yes," his aunt said. "Your mom called me soon after she climbed out of the river."

Ethan closed his eyes as a flood of emotion roared through his head. *Mom plunged off a bridge and crawled out of a wrecked, submerged car. Did someone really want her dead? We had her funeral. She's alive.* He opened his eyes and stared at the road ahead. "Why didn't you tell me?"

"Believe me, that was the hardest thing I have ever done. I know it was even harder for your mother. For her safety, and for yours, we thought it would be best if she laid low. You know, pretended to be dead. Those men aren't fooling around. I was able to provide her with a small amount of cash and one change of clothes, but that was all we could risk. I know how hard these last three weeks were for you, Ethan. So many times I wanted to tell you. Your mother and I realized how persistent these guys could be. That made us even more determined to stick to our plan. Your mom had to wait. An early return was too dangerous."

"Well, you were right about them being persistent. They waited three weeks, and now they found her."

"Yes. They really want what is in your green bag." Before long, the van pulled into a tiny parking lot. "We're here."

Ethan's mom ran toward the van. Ethan had always enjoyed the warmth of his mom's hug, but never so much as now, after he had thought she was gone forever. To feel her breathe, to smell her hair, to touch her felt like a tiny glimpse of heaven. Ethan didn't care a bit that he was crying. When his mother finally released her grip, she looked around anxiously before instructing everyone to get inside. Only then did Ethan notice that she had cut her curly brown hair short and wasn't wearing makeup. He didn't care. She looked wonderful.

The motel room was small but clean. Along with the typical double bed and nightstand, the room included a small television and an uncomfortable-looking chair pulled up to a round table. The bathroom was next to the door.

"Hello, Geneva. And Raymond," Ethan's mom said. "I hate to ask, but why are you here?"

"Actually, I'm babysitting," said Gen.

"Worst babysitter ever," Raymond said. "So far today I have been subjected to numerous public displays of affection—"

"Raymond . . ." groaned Gen.

"That's fine," Ethan's mom said. "I'm thrilled that my son is hanging out with someone who is going to change the world someday."

"—And," Raymond continued, "I was exposed to dangerous criminals. I'm glad that Ethan was with us to help us escape. So there is a bright side."

Abi's happy expression drained away. "I guess I'm not surprised that they went after you." She wiped her eyes. "Does anyone else know you're here?"

Ethan shook his head.

"Good. Trust no one."

"What about Dad?"

"I don't know." She paused after saying it, as if in deep thought. "Now, tell me what happened back home."

"I'm not entirely sure, Mom. All I know is that someone wants you, or whatever is in this bag."

Ethan placed the green baseball bag on the table and took out the burlap bundle. "We thought you were dead. We had a funeral. Three weeks later you call and tell me to get something hidden in the closet. These two men, who apparently have been watching me for quite some time, got tired of waiting. They kicked in our front and back door and chased us through the house. We got out through the attic. Then Aunt Shelly picked us up and brought us here. So why is this thing so important?"

His mom sighed. "You've been through a lot, Ethan. I'm sorry."

"We all have," Ethan said. "We would just like some explanation."

"I'll try, but I still don't understand a lot of it myself. As you know, not quite a month ago, your father called me out of the blue. I hadn't spoken to him for months. Well, he was excited about the old bones that his crew uncovered. To him they looked like dinosaur bones. Turns out he was right. One of them was particularly interesting, so he carefully removed that particular bone from the site before anyone else noticed.

You might find this surprising, but at times your father is not a complete idiot."

"Is that what this is?" asked Gen, pointing to the bundle.

"This is it," Abi said as she started to carefully peel away the duct tape. All eyes were on the bundle on the table. Curiosity grew as each length of duct tape was removed. By the time the tape was gone and the burlap was unrolled, everyone was leaning in to get a good look. On the table lay a large, dingy-white bone. The bone measured approximately three feet long and about six inches in diameter, with rounded knobs on both ends. Most of the surfaces were clean, with some dirt and grit still filling in the grooves and pits.

"Is it a real dinosaur bone?" Ethan asked.

"Actually, it's a fossil. The old bone has been replaced by minerals perfectly preserving it."

"What's this sticking into the bone?" Gen asked. "Is it glass?"

"Not glass, but obsidian," Abi said.

"I know obsidian," Raymond said, jumping in. "In school we learned that obsidian is a really hard black stone that is so shiny you can almost see your reflection. This kind of rock is formed when you have rapidly cooling lava."

"Looks like a spearhead," Ethan said.

"I believe it is a spearhead," Abi said. "Obsidian was used frequently to make arrow points and spearheads. The stone was easy to sharpen and could really hold an edge."

"I get it," Ethan said. "So some caveman dude stuck his spear into this dinosaur. That must have been a battle. How big was this thing?"

"Even though I haven't worked in the field for a number of years, I am fairly certain this bone is from an allosaurus. This particular dinosaur could grow to over thirty feet in length, possibly more. Each stood fifteen feet tall and weighed over two tons. Compared to a person, this one was huge, a monster, a behemoth."

"OK," Ethan said, "but the bigger they are, the harder they fall. I'm guessing this dino was probably just a slow-moving plant eater."

"Guess again. He was a fast-moving carnivore. An allosaurus had dozens of razor sharp teeth and huge claws for grabbing and holding their prey. Their tail alone could probably knock over a tree. This was no T. rex, but I wouldn't want to be the one poking it with a sharp stick."

"Whoa, that caveman must have been either really hungry or incredibly stupid," Ethan said. "Maybe a group of hunters chased it and cornered it. Maybe they had a net. They could have stabbed this thing many times before it escaped. What an awesome battle that would have been."

"Not awesome at all," Gen said. "That battle could never have taken place. Dinosaurs and humans were separated by millions of years. That's what we've been taught."

Ethan shrugged. "OK, I guess that's right. Maybe some guy found this bone and used it for target practice or something."

"That was my first thought," Abi said. "But look closer. See the odd formation around the spear point? That is new bone growth."

Raymond leaned in to get a closer look. "New bone growth. The wound was healing. That's how you know it was alive when it was stabbed."

"All right!" Ethan said. "We had a battle after all, except now the caveman dude has a very angry dinosaur on his hands—and no spear."

"Mrs. Booker, everyone will say this is impossible," Gen said.

Abi paused, taking a long hard look at the fossil. "Not everyone, Gen. It's only impossible to those who are afraid of the truth."

Ethan strained to follow the discussion. Gen was right. In school they had all been taught that dinosaurs and humans did not live at the same time. The only logical way for a single-cell organism to become a complex animal would be through evolution over billions of years. Ethan remembered a timeline posted in the front of his science class. Dinosaurs were placed somewhere around the middle, with humans appearing at the very end.

Ethan backed away from the fossil. "Forget about that for now. What happened to you after you brought it home?"

"That first day was incredible. In my hands, I was holding this amazing discovery. I have never been so excited in my life. I needed to share it with someone I could trust. Joseph was the first one I thought of. He was a brilliant student I had a few years back in my class. That very night after you left for your date with Gen, I drove to his house. Joseph verified my findings and shared in the excitement. I came back home and hid the fossil in our closet while trying to figure out the best way to present it. I must admit, along with the thrill of this discovery, I found myself happy to talk to your father again. I really didn't expect that."

"But this was entirely his fault, Mom," Ethan blurted. "You know it was. He doesn't care about you. All he cares about is money. He used you. He wanted to know if the fossil had any real value. Obviously, he will do anything to get it back."

Ethan's mom paused and took a deep breath. "As I was saying, this was a remarkable find. Every scientist hopes to one day stumble upon something that will advance our understanding of the world."

"Mrs. Booker," Gen said, "this fossil could completely alter our thinking."

"Lots of people believe that dinosaurs and humans lived at the same time," Raymond said. "We talked about it at church, so I wrote a report on it for school. For instance, did you know that stories about dragons exist in nearly every part of the world? Weird, isn't it? I mean, how did these different cultures separated by thousands of miles conjure up such similar details, unless they actually saw them?"

"But we're talking about dinosaurs, not dragons," Ethan said.

"I know, but the word 'dinosaur' wasn't even invented until the nineteenth century," Raymond answered.

Ethan grinned. "Oh, of course." Raymond was scary smart sometimes.

"There's other stuff, too," Raymond said. "For example, there's this carving in a Cambodian temple that looks like a stegosaurus."

"I've seen it," Ethan's mom said. "That carving does resemble a stegosaurus. But you have to understand, today's scientists begin with the worldview that dinosaurs lived millions of years before humans came onto the scene. For a person to see a stegosaurus walking around and carve its image into a wall would be impossible. Therefore, it cannot be a stegosaurus."

"Or," said Raymond, "someone saw a stegosaurus tromping through the jungle, thought it was cool, and carved it in a wall."

"Sure," Abi said. "But suggest that possibility to the scientific community, and you would face a lifetime of ridicule."

"No kidding," Raymond said. "I got a D-minus on my report."

Ethan stared at the bone and the spearhead. "You should have gotten a better grade."

Gen spoke up. "Mrs. Booker, what happened to you after you hid the fossil?"

"Joseph called me while I was at Ethan's baseball game. He sounded troubled, and I couldn't understand everything he was trying to say. However, I understood that he needed to see me. When I got to his house, things didn't feel right. I began to worry about his safety. I sat in my car, trying to figure out what to do. That's when two men attacked me, trying to get me out of the car. That whole afternoon is still a blur, but the next thing I remember, some car was trying to run me off the road. Twice I was rammed from behind. I was terrified and drove even faster.

"The third time he rammed me, I completely lost control. My car spun through the railing and flipped off the bridge, right into the middle of the river. I'm not clear on exactly what happened next. I'm sure I was in shock. I remember being wet and cold and disoriented. I didn't know which way was up, and I couldn't breathe. Somehow I unbuckled my seat belt. My door was open, and I just floated away from the car, down the river. When I climbed onto the riverbank, I was quite a ways downstream. I hid behind some trees and looked back upstream. All I could see of my car were two of the wheels barely sticking out of the water. Two men had already jumped in the river and were all over the car. They kept diving down, coming back up, looking for me, and looking for the fossil. They were angry, to say the least. I decided to let them believe I was dead."

Ethan's mom was visibly shaking, her face quite pale. Ethan put his arms around her. "Who would do this?"

"Could be someone who wants to sell the fossil for millions of dollars," Raymond said.

"I bet you're right," Ethan said.

"Or, it could be what you said, Mrs. Booker," Gen offered.

"Remind me."

"You said, 'It's only impossible to those who are afraid of the truth.' Perhaps the person behind this is some powerful person who benefits from the status quo and doesn't want to see it all unraveled."

"Wait," Ethan said. "Are you saying that someone tried to kill my mother because they can't deal with the truth about dinosaurs?"

Abi picked up the fossil. "Whoever it is, they're afraid. Afraid of getting cornered by the truth. They're in a battle, doing the very same thing this dinosaur was trying to do."

"What's that, Mom?"

"Survive."

The thought was disturbing. Ethan stared at the fossil. The implications were mind-boggling. *Someone with a lot of power is threatened by this fossil.*

"There could be another battle," Ethan said.

"Could be a big one," Abi said. "I believe this behemoth is quite powerful."

After a slight pause in the conversation, Gen whispered to Ethan. "Can I talk to you outside?"

Ethan looked at his mom, who nodded her approval.

∞ ∞ ∞ ∞ ∞ ∞ ∞

The night air felt cool but moist. With a breeze off the ocean, the smell of salt, sand, and nettle was wonderful.

They walked a bit before Ethan spoke, "What's up?"

"I'm really worried about your mom. I can't imagine how hard these past few weeks have been for her. Now she has to worry about us."

"She seems to be doing OK."

"She is an amazing woman, but as strong as your mom is, this whole fossil thing is a huge burden for her. What if she decides that our safety is more important than the fossil?"

"That is her decision. If I had to choose between an old fossil and you, I think I'd pick you."

"That's very sweet."

"Heck, if I had to choose between the fossil and Raymond, I might even choose Raymond."

"You should have quit while you were ahead," Gen said with a weak smile. "Here's the thing. I know your mom is worried, Ethan. But I have this feeling—"

"Here it comes, another one of your intuitions."

"Deal with it, Ethan. I have this feeling that maybe, just *maybe*, everything is going to turn out fine. For whatever reason, we are part of something unique, something extraordinary. What happened to your mother was horrible. I know how awful it was for you. Despite that, I cannot help but feel that this is all for good. That fossil very well may be more important than you or I."

"You're freaking me out, Gen. I hate it when you do this."

"Do what?"

"This 'I have a feeling' stuff."

"Sorry."

"Where does that come from, anyway? I suppose you're going to say it comes from God."

"That's the way He made me, Ethan."

"Well, I pretty much dig the way He made you—most of you anyway."

"Once again, you come so close to saying something sweet."

They walked quietly for a while. "What are you asking me to do?"

"I know your mom is trained as a scientist, but more than that, she is your mother. She knows the importance of the fossil, but I'm concerned that at some point she will put our safety ahead of the fossil. I completely understand how she feels. But . . ."

"But what?" Ethan asked.

Gen hesitated. She appeared to be gathering her thoughts. "I really feel that this is bigger than just us. Perhaps God is providing a chance for people to become reacquainted with the truth. The hardest thing to do in the world is change someone's viewpoint. This fossil has the power to do just that, Ethan. We can't give up the fossil, Ethan. It's ours to protect."

Ethan did not respond. They turned and walked back toward the motel. Gen reached for Ethan's hand. Such a simple thing, holding hands. Why did it make his heart nearly beat through his chest? Much too quickly, they were back.

Ethan stopped before going in, looking directly into her eyes. "It's not that I doubt you, Gen, or your intuition. But Mom might decide to give up and go to the police. I'm really not sure what I'll do. Those idiot criminals already ran her off a bridge. Mom is not going to take any unnecessary risks with us around."

"She shouldn't," Gen said. "But sometimes you have to face risks, the ones that are necessary."

Ethan looked at the hotel room door. He was in no hurry to go inside.

"Can I talk to you about something else?" Gen asked.

"Sure," Ethan said. In reality, he was happy to have any excuse to stay outside longer with Gen.

"Something is bothering me," she said. "My faith."

Ethan was on shaky ground here and would never think to initiate a conversation about God with Gen. Now he had no choice.

"I don't understand," Ethan managed to say.

"I've been thinking about your mom's fossil. It's very convicting. The more I think about it, the worse I feel. I really let God down."

Ethan had two options. He could either admit that he had no idea what Gen was talking about, or he could just listen. This time, he wisely chose to listen.

"A dinosaur is described in the Bible, in the book of Job. Since I have been told my whole life that dinosaurs and humans never coexisted, I just ignored that part. I suppose I have also ignored other parts mainly because I didn't like them. Other parts of the Bible I like a lot. They are amazing and life-changing. So basically, I have been picking and choosing which parts pleased me, which parts suited my view."

"Why is that bad?" Ethan asked. "Do you really think it has to be an all-or-nothing deal?"

"Yeah, maybe I do. I know that view isn't what our culture wants to hear. We're supposed to think that total commitment and real devotion are foolish and fanatical. That's the worldview today. To be spiritual is fine and acceptable. People like being spiritual. They feel good, similar to the feeling they have when they donate money to the local animal shelter. Society pats them on the back and says, 'You are a good person.' You know what it is, Ethan? It's a trap."

Ethan was totally lost.

Gen continued. "Your mother said, 'This behemoth could be very powerful.' She's right. I think whoever—or whatever—this behemoth is, it is so powerful that it tries to control what we believe to be true. But for some reason, our little fossil is a very real threat."

Once again, Ethan knew that Gen was way out of his league.

"You know what really bugs me?" Gen said. "I had to see it with my own eyes. I had to have proof, like Thomas, the disciple who doubted Jesus was actually alive even though He stood right in front of him. That fossil helped me recognize just how wrong I have been. We think we are so smart. We think our intellect is supreme."

Just then Ethan's mom stuck her head out the door. "Hey, you two, it's getting late, and I haven't seen my son for three weeks."

Back inside, Raymond and Shelly sat on the bed watching a *Star Trek* rerun. Raymond was arguing with Ethan's aunt. "You're wrong. Not all Klingons are bad. Worf is a good Klingon. He's even part of the crew in *Star Trek Next Generation*."

"That doesn't count. In the original series, all the Klingons are bad," Shelly countered.

Ethan's head was swimming in thoughts. *What a surreal ending to an unreal day.* Breakfast with his aunt seemed like years ago. Everything since then was a blur, except for one thing: *Mom was alive!*

CHAPTER SEVEN

Evolution is the greatest engine of atheism ever invented.

— William B. Provine[5]

David walked up the three cracked cement steps to the front door of the small old house near the edge of town. He knocked loudly on the wooden door. No one came to the door, but David was certain that someone was home. He knocked again, harder.

Finally a voice shouted from inside. "Go away, there's no one here."

"Joseph? Is this the home of Joseph Nori?" David asked.

After a short pause. "Maybe."

"Joseph, my name is David Booker. I'm here to talk with you about Abi—Dr. Abigail Booker."

Now the pause was much longer. Finally, David heard a series of clicks and clunks from the door as locks and deadbolts were opened. Joseph let David inside without saying a word. Joseph stuck his head outside briefly, looking one way, then the next, before shutting and re-locking the door.

David was surprised at Joseph's appearance. Although they had never met, he remembered Abi describing him as neat, handsome, and always smiling. The man before him shared none of those characteristics. His hair was a ridiculous pile on his head, he badly needed a shave, his clothes were wrinkled and dirty, like the rest of the room, and he looked as though he hadn't smiled in a long time.

"Joseph. I'm so glad to meet you. I'm Abi's husband."

"She is divorced. You must be an ex-husband," Joseph corrected.

"Yes, I was her husband." David's voice trailed off.

"I don't want you to be here," Joseph interrupted. "I happen to know that you hurt her very badly. She was a wonderful person. She was a wonderful teacher and brilliant scientist. Now she is dead, and I will not talk about it with anyone. Please go, Mr. Booker."

"Joseph, please," David said. "Abi trusted you. I know she did."

"There is nothing to talk about!" Joseph said. He walked to the door.

"I have reason to believe that she's alive," David said.

Joseph turned away from the door, his eyes wide open. "What did you say?"

"After work last night, I drove to her house to check on Ethan, my son. The front and back doors had been demolished, completely removed from their hinges. My son's bedroom was a total wreck. His door was smashed in, and the attic ceiling had collapsed into the middle of his room. Ethan was nowhere to be found."

"I am so very sorry to hear this. I believe I am familiar with the men who may have done this. They tied me up and forced me to call Dr. Booker."

"I found a few small broken branches under an open attic window. I know it's not much, but I think he climbed out the window while his pursuers were busy crashing through the ceiling."

"You should call the authorities," Joseph said.

"I did. I told them that my son is missing and may be in danger, as well as my wife. But those guys believe that Abigail is dead. Since they're not concerned about her, they refused to take me seriously."

"You still have not explained why you think she is alive," Joseph said.

"It's all about that fossil, Joseph."

"I know nothing at all about any fossil. I will not say anything about that."

"Wow," David said. "They got to you too, didn't they? OK, I'll talk. Whoever these people are, they are after the fossil. I'm guessing the black market for something as unique as our fossil would be huge. They couldn't care less about Abi or you or anyone. They just want the fossil"

"Once again," Joseph said, "why are you saying that Dr. Booker is alive?"

David closed his eyes and bit his lip. "Perhaps I'm a pathetic man grasping at nothing. But see if you think this is plausible. Why would they break into her house? One day after the bone is dug out of the ground, two things happen. First, her house is searched. They find nothing, so they go after Abi. Second, her car goes over the bridge. All of this happens in a very short time. They work fast because there must be a large amount of money at stake. To me that makes sense. If Abi is dead, then the whereabouts of the fossil died with her. Nothing more can be done."

Joseph sat down on the nearby sofa. He said nothing. David moved slowly across the room, collecting his thoughts. He found a chair on the opposite side of the room and bent forward to explain the rest of his theory.

"But then, nothing—for three weeks. Suddenly, boom, they break down two doors to get into her house. This was clearly not a robbery. No one robs a home that is occupied. They were not after the fossil because they had already searched the house earlier. They were intent on kidnapping

Ethan. Why would they want Ethan? I can think of only one reason. I would be willing to bet my life that Abigail survived. Somehow they found out. Ethan may not know where the fossil is, but he might just know the whereabouts of his mother. The bad guys are after Ethan because Ethan knows about his mother."

Joseph said nothing for a long time. His face seemed to brighten a bit with the possibility that Abi could be alive. Finally he said, "I agree with you, but I think you are wrong."

"What?"

"I agree with your logic. You are wrong about the value of the fossil."

"Why?" David asked. "I only said the value on the black market could be huge."

"Yes," Joseph said. "But from what I have seen, the value of the fossil cannot be measured in dollars."

David looked straight at the young man. "So, she *did* show it to you."

Joseph stiffened. His eyes narrowed. "Why are you here?"

"Because I need your help. I know you can find her," David said.

"Why don't you ask her sister? Shelly might know where she is," Joseph said.

David hesitated. "Shelly doesn't trust me."

"Shelly is smart like her sister. I don't think I trust you either. Maybe you too just want the fossil."

"Oh, come on, Joseph. How does that make any sense? I'm the one who gave it to her in the first place."

"Yes," Joseph said. "But that was before you realized its value. Now suddenly you want it back. Maybe you were the one who broke down her doors. I doubt you had a key."

David would have gotten angry if a sudden flood of hopelessness hadn't swept over him. He held his face in his hands and wiped his eyes. "I'm not sure what you think of me. My life has been a mess for two years. I divorced Abi for a woman who left me four months later. I drank too much and gambled too much. Do you know what happened to me, Joseph? I thought I was important. Obviously, when you are *important*, you deserve the best. I had plenty of money to spend on better friends, better parties, and better cars. I thought my life was rich. But in these last two years, I have finally realized that the only thing of value I ever had was my family."

David paused to clear his throat and wipe his eyes. He looked at Joseph. *Did Joseph believe him, or did Joseph feel like he was watching an impressive performance? Did Joseph see that these emotions were from the heart? To David, Joseph had to. He had to convince Joseph of his sincerity.*

David was able to continue. "If there's only the tiniest chance to get them back, I have to take it. All I want is to see Abi alive. Joseph, please, you must trust me. It may be our only chance."

Joseph hesitated. "If you have any real connection with Abi and your son, you already know a safe place where they would meet."

CHAPTER EIGHT

A liar begins with making falsehood appear like truth, and ends with making truth itself appear like falsehood.

—William Shenstone[6]

E ven though the room was small, everyone found a place to rest. Abi, Shelly, and Gen crowded onto the bed. Raymond slept in the tub. Ethan tried to sleep in the stiff-backed, saggy-bottom chair, but soon gave up. Not only was the chair hopelessly uncomfortable, his mind kept racing. Beyond the revelation that he once again had a mother, other events tumbled around in his head. *Why is my dad asking all these questions about the bone? Who are the two men that broke into our house? Who hired them? Is Gen as into me as I am in to her?*

He silently grabbed his aunt's keys and slipped outside. He hoped he could find a place in the van to fall asleep. He slid the passenger door open without making a sound, and shut it as quietly as he could. He opened one window just enough so he could listen to the ocean. The third-row bench seat was nearly long enough and looked to be a major upgrade from the hotel room chair. By bending his knees and hanging his feet off the end, he was reasonably comfortable. The moonlight coming in the side windows and the smell of the ocean made his new bed tolerable. He remembered a time of sleeping in a tent with his mom and dad by the shore. He lay very still, hoping to hear the waves. Instead, he heard footsteps.

Ethan was completely exposed as the footsteps moved quickly toward the moonlit van. Without a sound Ethan rolled off the seat and slid underneath the bench seat as far as he could. The steel rod jabbing him in the back turned out to be a tire iron. Ethan reached back, clutching it tightly. The footsteps stopped by the side of the van. Ethan could only assume the person belonging to the footsteps was looking inside. For a long time, Ethan heard nothing. Finally the steps moved away from the van and headed straight for the motel room door. The motel was reflected in the side window. He could see a solitary figure attempting to look into the darkened window of the room. Then the figure turned quickly and left.

So much for getting a good night's sleep. The rest of the night Ethan stayed awake and on guard, clutching the tire iron. Watching. Listening.

At seven in the morning, Ethan released his grip on the tire iron and limped back to the room. His aunt was dressed and ready to head out the door.

"What's up?" Ethan asked.

"I'm going on a vacation," Shelly answered. "I'm taking a Greyhound bus. The station is just a five-minute walk from here."

Ethan agreed that this was actually a good idea. Up to this point Aunt Shelly's involvement with her sister had been minimal. Still, it would be better that his aunt not go home right away. This would provide her with an extra amount of detachment, and her sister with wheels. On the other hand, Gen and Raymond were completely involved and likely identifiable to the men chasing them. If they left with Shelly, they might endanger her. And returning home would be far too dangerous for them. This seemed like the right decision—his Aunt Shelly would leave, and Gen and Raymond would stay with Ethan and his mom. They must have discussed all this during the night.

"I'll see you soon," Shelly said as she gave Ethan an unusually big hug.

"Thanks, Aunt Shelly, for everything," Ethan said before she quickly walked away.

"Raymond," Gen said, "get out of the tub. I need a shower."

"I need to eat," Ethan said. "All you highly evolved smart people stay here and figure out a plan. I'll head out and try to stab something with my spear."

"Try the convenience store over on the next block," his mom said. "Better yet, I'll go. I need to stretch my legs."

"I'd rather you stayed here, Mom. I don't want to lose you again."

"Well, thanks, Ethan. And I appreciate that. By the way, I've been meaning to ask you guys kind of a tough question for me: how was the funeral?"

"It was beautiful," Gen said. "Yellow roses were everywhere. The organist played some wonderful songs, including 'Amazing Grace.' Ethan said it is one of your favorites."

"It sounds lovely. Sorry I missed it," Abi said with a slight smile.

Ethan just shook his head at the absurd conversation and headed out the door. At least everyone was in good spirits. No need to tell them about his overnight visitor. The lone figure walking around last night may have just been a bum or a voyeur or some innocent passerby out for a walk.

Ethan jogged past the familiar park where his family spent many summer days. Everything was as he remembered: the same fire pits to roast hot dogs and s'mores, the same tiny baseball diamond to play Wiffle ball, and the same wonderful beach. Ethan smiled as he remembered skipping stones far across the water with his dad. The convenience store was the same store where Ethan's dad had purchased snacks and other goodies for their picnics in those happier times.

Inside the store, Ethan grabbed a plastic basket and immediately started filling it up with apples, beef jerky, bread, peanut butter, milk, and bottled water. He set that basket down at the register and went back for more. This time he bagged carrots, crackers, cheese, and two cans of Pringles. The burritos were tempting, but he didn't remember seeing a microwave in the room. He paid in cash and filled four plastic shopping bags.

Ethan found it amusing that despite the fact he was running on zero sleep and had two hit men hunting for him, he was in a really good mood. Of course, the fact that his mom was alive helped. Another positive was all the quality time with Gen. Even her little brother Raymond was fun to have around. On top of that, he liked taking care of everyone. That felt good.

Everything changed the moment he pushed open the heavy glass door of the store and stepped outside. Ethan could see the two men standing by their car. The man with the icy voice and blond crew cut cleared his throat loudly before holding his cell phone to his ear. The other man wasn't paying attention to anything except the beach. Ethan quickly walked out of the store and around the corner. He leaned against the wall and peered back at them.

"Yeah, we're in town now," Frost said with his loud whisper-voice. "Yeah, I know. Well, right now we need to get something to eat. Of course. We'll take care of it."

He placed the phone in his pocket and spoke to his partner. "Broderick, they've been spotted at a motel a couple of blocks from here. The same van that picked them up outside the house was parked there all night. This should be as easy as pie."

He suddenly turned to look around. Ethan pressed himself close to the wall.

"You wait here by the car," he said. "I need to get something to eat."

"Boss, grab me some Ho Hos, would ya?" said the other man. "Can ya hurry? I gotta take a leak."

"Ho Hos?"

"Yeah, don't take too long."

Ethan remained hidden until Frost entered the store. Ethan peeked around the corner of the building. The other man was extremely antsy, wiggling back and forth like a little boy. Finally, he gave in. He cursed and dashed into the store.

Ethan knew he had to hurry. He ran to the car. Luckily, the doors were unlocked. Ethan reached in under the dashboard and released the hood. He located the distributor cap and immediately yanked the top wire free. Carefully, he lowered the hood, shutting it without a sound. He grabbed his four bags of groceries and literally flew to the motel.

"Gotta go," he called out as soon as he burst into the room.

"What is it?" Gen asked.

"Now!" Ethan insisted. "I'll explain when we're in the van!"

They grabbed their clothes, gathered up the fossil, and bolted for the van. Ethan tossed the groceries inside and took the driver's seat. He started the van and drove as fast as he could without speeding. For now, the direction didn't matter.

"I gave us a slight head start, but it won't last long."

"Was it whisper guy and his buddy?" Raymond asked.

"Yeah. They were in the parking lot at the store. They'll have a hard time starting their car, but I'm sure they'll figure it out."

"This has gone too far," Ethan's mom said. "Those animals will stop at nothing, and I will not endanger you kids any longer. Ethan, take a left here and drive downtown to the police station."

"Wait," Gen said. "Let's just think this through. If we go to the police we will have to tell them everything. We will have to explain about the bone and give it to them as evidence. Likely we will never see it again, especially if the person looking for the fossil is as powerful as we think. Once we hand it over, the bone may disappear for good."

"I don't care anymore," Abi insisted. "It's just a fossil. Nothing is more important than you."

Gen reached forward, touching Ethan on the shoulder. Ethan realized this was her signal for him to push the issue.

"I think Gen is right, Mom. Let's not throw in the towel just yet."

Ethan looked in his rearview mirror to see if Gen approved. She did.

"We know for a fact that this fossil is incredibly important," Gen said. "Perhaps even miraculous. I'm all for being safe, and believe it or not, I am trying to be responsible for Raymond. I'm just asking, do we have any other options? Is there anyone nearby that you trust?

Ethan's mom sighed. She hesitated. "There is one person. In grad school I had a professor named Dr. Emery. He knows more about dinosaurs and reconstructing prehistoric skeletons than anyone. Years ago we were working together on a dig in New Guinea. During our excavation of a prehistoric turtle near our camp, I uncovered the most amazing spirit mask. Spirit masks were used by the Kamoro tribe in secret ceremonies to drive spirits to the land of the dead. This mask was in excellent condition, and I was familiar with at least twenty museums that would pay thousands to add it to their collection.

"However, Dr. Emery stepped forward and explained that those masks were sacred and rightfully belonged to the Kamoro people. We walked six miles in the middle of the day just to hand it to the elder of the tribe. That impressed me. That was over twenty years ago, but at that time I had never met a more ethical scientist." She stopped and looked troubled.

"Is there more?" Ethan asked.

"Like I said, that was a long time ago. I have only met with him a couple of times in the last ten years. Dr. Emery had become the preeminent authority on reconstructive paleontology. If you had a question about what bone went where, you would ask Dr. Emery. No one doubted his decisions or his knowledge. All the same, he seems to have changed. Possibly his age has affected his thinking.

"Last time I talked to him, he hardly listened to me; he seemed obsessed with his skeletons. I know for a fact he has become quite wealthy, serving as a consultant and board member to numerous universities and museums. However, he didn't seem to enjoy his money; he just worked on his dinosaurs. I'm not sure he enjoyed that either—yet he immersed himself in his skeletons. To me it was as though he was trying to escape from something. I don't know. He is a different man than I knew all those years ago. I can't say that I trust him completely, but he's our best bet. So, it's either Dr. Emery or the police."

"Dr. Emery it is," Gen said.

Ethan looked at his mom. Obviously, she would have been happier going to the police. "Are you OK with this?"

"I appreciate what you and Gen are doing," she said. "The fossil is a significant discovery. In a way, I am responsible for it. The bone disappearing while in my possession would be a tragedy. On the other hand, nothing is as important as you and Gen and Raymond. Dr. Emery is where this ends."

"That's where it ends, I promise," Ethan said. "I like that option better than handing it to the police. So, where are we going?"

"Keep going straight ahead," she said. "When you get to the main freeway, head north to Seattle. Let's get ourselves to this museum; it's the Museum of Natural History."

"Actually, let's avoid the highway. Those two guys following us know what we're driving. We'll take the scenic route. What are the chances of you finding this Dr. Emery?"

"I'm pretty sure I can find him. Like I said, the man is obsessed. After lecturing at the university, he always heads to the museum, where he works late into the night categorizing fossils and recreating skeletons. He just cannot get enough of it. We'll find him there."

∞ ∞ ∞ ∞ ∞ ∞ ∞

Later that day, David exited the office at a small motel near Seaside Park. He walked quickly toward his silver Buick. Joseph sat in the passenger seat.

"They may have been here," David said as he slid in behind the wheel. "You were right, Joseph. I needed to trust my instincts."

"You said 'may have been here.' You are not certain?"

"The name on the register was Smith. They paid for the room in cash. The hotel manager said they were traveling in a yellow van. Her sister drives a yellow van. That would be their likely means of transportation since Ethan's car is still back home in the garage."

"Yes," Joseph said. "That must be them."

"But the manager said five people slept in the room last night. Five. He said there were two women, one younger man—possibly a teenager . . . one younger woman—again, possibly a teen—and one very young boy. I did see Ethan hanging out with Geneva and Raymond the other day, but why would they have come here with Shelly and Ethan? I can't imagine Abi would involve those other kids."

"Unless she had no other choice," Joseph said.

David thought about this. The yellow van, paying in cash, "Smith"—all these things fit. The size of the group didn't entirely make sense.

"At this point, we have to assume the group that stayed here last night included Abi and Ethan. If it wasn't them, we have completely lost their trail. So Joseph, where will they go next?"

"Do you have state or area maps?" Joseph asked.

"Yeah. Open the glove box."

Joseph found a Washington state map neatly folded in David's glove compartment. He studied it for some time.

"I have a guess," Joseph said.

"Good. Tell me where we should go," David said.

"I must remind you that this is simply a guess. I truly have no clear idea where they might be headed."

"Where, Joseph?" David insisted.

Joseph paused and looked at the map again. "I believe we should drive to Seattle."

"Seattle?" repeated David as he started the car. "Fine with me. I'm sure you have a theory about Seattle. Want to share it with me?"

"Of course," Joseph said, now smiling and enjoying the idea of being able to help rescue his former professor, who he respected so much, from trouble. "If I were Dr. Booker, I would head to Seattle. Specifically, I would go to the Museum of Natural History. This museum is known for its work in archaeology and paleontology. There is one particular scientist with his own personal lab right there in the museum. I can't recall his name, but he is a very important man in the world of paleontology. If in fact I were travelling with a group of young people, I would be very concerned for their safety. After all, dangerous men are trying to take the fossil. The best solution would be to get the fossil to this museum. I believe Dr. Booker has a history of working with this man and trusts him. Get to the museum, deliver the fossil, and the dangerous men will leave them alone."

David smiled as he pulled onto the highway. "That's quite a theory, Joseph. I like it. I'm especially glad she can trust this scientist, whoever he is."

"Oh no, this man cannot be trusted," Joseph said.

"But you just said—"

"I simply said that *Dr. Booker* trusts him."

"You said once she gives him the fossil, she would be safe," David said.

Joseph paused, as though he was organizing his thoughts. "I explained my theory on where Dr. Booker might go and why she might go to the museum. In no way did I indicate the outcome should she decide to go there."

"What are you saying?" David asked.

"I'm saying I wouldn't trust this scientist with a ten-foot probing stick. Perhaps at one time he was a genuine human being. When I met him he was distant, as if controlled, or at least motivated by, something outside of his soul. If they are going to the Seattle Museum, I believe they are still in trouble," Joseph said. "In fact, they may be headed, as you would say, straight into the lion's den."

David grimaced and pushed harder on the gas pedal.

"Now I remember," Joseph said. "His name is Dr. Emery."

CHAPTER NINE

You think you are too intelligent to believe in God. I am not like you.

—Napoleon Bonaparte

Ethan parked the van in a lot directly across the street from the Museum of Natural History. His mother carefully placed the fossil inside the sport bag once again. She threw the strap over her shoulder to carry it inside. After a collective deep breath, the group headed inside.

The structure was impressive. Massive pillars framed the marble steps to the entrance. Small concrete statues depicting reptiles, fish, and birds mingled artistically in and out of the pillars, leading the way into the building.

It was already late afternoon. The young lady behind the desk indicated that the museum would close soon and kindly provided her opinion that paying full price was a bit foolish. Nevertheless, she shrugged and handed them their tickets. However, before they passed through the turnstiles, the museum guard stopped them.

"Sorry, ma'am, but no bags are allowed inside."

"It's OK, sir," Ethan said. "She's . . . uh . . ."

"She's what?" the guard asked.

"She's . . . incontinent," Ethan whispered to the guard.

Abi gave her son a look that could only be described as a combination of utter mortification mixed with complete admiration. "Oopsie," she said, shrugging the guard's way to play up her newfound diagnosis.

"That's all right, Mom. We brought along plenty of extras." Ethan smiled and patted the bag.

The guard was simultaneously confused and revolted. Not sure what to do, he let them walk right in.

"I'll get you for that one, Ethan," Abi whispered after they were beyond the guard. "Someday you'll pay dearly."

With Raymond snickering behind them, the group moved to the museum's prehistoric section. "Dr. Emery always arrives just before closing. If my guess is right, this whole thing will be over soon," Abi assured them.

"I'll be glad to go home," Raymond said. It was one of the first times in the last couple of days the kid had said something serious.

"I'll watch for him. You three, try to act normal," Abi said.

The prehistoric display was big, but Ethan had expected something even more impressive. Dozens of glass cases displaying fossils and other artifacts filled the room. Lining the walls were many elaborate posters describing the evolutionary process. One of the posters depicted the classic progression of a monkey-like thing on all fours . . . gradually transforming to an upright, intelligent human.

Raymond stood in front of a fully constructed, small-but-ferocious-looking raptor skeleton. "I thought this place was famous for dinosaurs. They only have one."

"A larger exhibit would take up too much room. This is a small museum, Raymond. Dr. Emery is directly responsible for categorizing, constructing, and shipping dinosaur skeletons to museums around the world. He is extremely well connected. It's his life. He lectures at the university during the day, and then he comes here to work late into the night. I'm not exaggerating when I say that his work is never done.

"Most people don't know this, but whenever some new fossil or new information is uncovered, scientists often have to change their exhibits. The Carnegie Museum of Natural History in Pittsburgh had one of the biggest collections of reconstructed dinosaurs. Dr. Emery was very involved with that display. In 2007, they decided to dismantle the entire collection."

"You mean they took all the skeletons apart?" Raymond asked.

"That's correct," Abi answered. "Recent discoveries determined that the skeletons had been pieced together incorrectly."

"That's hilarious," Ethan said. "How could they get it wrong?"

"Try to be fair, Ethan," Abi said. "These things don't come with an instruction manual."

"So they changed what they believed to be the truth?" Gen asked.

"People forget that paleontologists are simply taking whatever evidence they find and using that to make an educated guess. Too often the world views the results of their work as fact. The truth is, modern ideas concerning dinosaurs change every day. Of course, usually those changes are small. The one in this bag just happens to be a doozy."

"Hey, look at this." Raymond was looking at a display called The Anasazi: Prehistoric Indians. "Says here, these Indians lived in what we now call Utah."

"Fascinating," Ethan said, mimicking a yawn, not understanding why Raymond was at all interested.

"OK, but look at that photograph of one of their rock drawings."

Ethan leaned in to get a closer look at the drawing. He could not believe his eyes.

"It's a dinosaur, isn't it?" Raymond asked. "They drew a picture of a dinosaur on the side of a cliff. That's like the stegosaurus carving in my school report."

"Well, that drawing sure looks like a dinosaur," Ethan said. "What do they say about it?"

Raymond read the plaque aloud. "Drawings such as this are seen often in prehistoric cultures. Dinosaur-like creatures were depicted in carvings and statues. Scientists attribute their existence to ancient mythology or imaginative flights of fancy."

"Again, they're wrong," Ethan said. "How could someone imagine a dinosaur and draw it perfectly? I think the scientists are the ones with the imaginative flights of fancy."

Ethan shook his head as he walked back to the raptor. "But this guy is seriously nasty looking. You would really have to be hungry to stick a spear into that."

"Our dinosaur was quite a bit larger than that," Abi said. "Can you imagine hunting something like that? Buying hamburger from the grocery store is much easier."

Ethan started to read. "'Two hundred to one hundred-and-fifty million years ago.' Someone explain this to me. People were just not around two hundred million years ago. With radiocarbon dating, scientists can be pretty sure about the age of stuff. I can see why they think that dinos and man were not walking around at the same time. Am I the only one confused here?"

"Ethan," Raymond said, "how old was Adam?"

"What?"

"You know, Adam—the first man. How old do you think he was when God created him?"

"I don't know, maybe eighteen. I suppose, in order for him to survive, he'd have to be old enough to gather food and stuff like that."

"OK, and how many days old?"

"That's a trick question, Raymond. I know I haven't been to church for a while, but he was only one day old," Ethan said.

"Think about it. For Adam to survive when he was created, he would have to have been about eighteen years old on his first day. Maybe the earth was millions of years old on its first day of creation. Just a thought. The point is, there is a lot we really don't know."

"I swear, between you and your sister, my head is gonna explode."

Abi tapped Ethan's shoulder. "There he is."

A rather tall, distinguished-looking man walked briskly down the hall. Although he was completely bald, Professor Emery had an impressive silver goatee. Ethan figured him to be about seventy, but he appeared to be in excellent shape. He swung his briefcase as he walked and whistled some old tune. He disappeared through a small doorway at the end of the hallway marked "Stairs."

An announcement came on the speaker system. "Your attention, please. The Seattle Museum of Natural History will be closing in ten minutes. Please begin to make your way to the exit area. We hope you enjoyed your visit."

The few people remaining headed for the exit. Ethan saw the guard slowly move away from his post and start his rounds. A few people lingered at various displays. The guard moved in their direction, pointing toward the doors.

Another announcement. "The museum is closing for the day. Thank you for visiting."

As soon as the guard moved out of the hallway and into a side exhibit room, Abi led the group toward the stairs, and they descended quickly to the basement. A single light shone from a door window at the end of the hall.

"Does that mean the doctor is in?" Ethan asked quietly.

"That would be our professor," Abi whispered.

Ethan knocked on the door, cleared his throat, and then said loudly, "You don't know me, Dr. Emery. Uhhh, my name is Ethan Booker. I believe you knew my mother, Dr. Abigail Booker?"

After a long pause, the door slowly opened. The tall professor wore the standard white lab coat covered with some sort of gray dust. "I'm very sorry to hear about your mother, young man. She was a brilliant teacher."

"Thank you. That's, uh . . . very nice of you."

"What can I do for you, Mr. Booker?"

"Well, for starters, you can let us in." Ethan's mom, Gen, and Raymond appeared from behind a corner and quickly entered the room.

"Good to see you again, Dr. Emery. Lock the door, please." Ethan's mom smiled as she walked past the completely stunned man.

"I . . . I . . . Dr. Booker, I don't understand," he said. "You're alive."

Raymond rolled his eyes. "Jeepers, *I* could be a professor."

Ethan was dumbfounded by the room in front of him. As big as a school cafeteria, table after table was covered with bones. Many of the bones were arranged neatly and had tags hanging from them. Other bones were simply in piles. Two complete dinosaur skeletons were standing in the middle of this large room. One was large and looked something like a T. rex. Ethan assumed the other one was a stegosaurus.

"We need your help," Gen said. "Mrs. Booker said you were a person we could trust."

"Mm—Mrs. Booker?" stammered the professor, still trying to make sense of her appearance. I'm ff—flattered," he said, desperately attempting to compose himself. "I assume this has something to do with the unusual bone."

Ethan and Gen looked at each other uneasily. Suddenly a loud knock at the door broke the tension in the air. "Dr. Emery? We'll be locking up now. Everything all right?"

Dr. Emery motioned for everyone to duck under a table. He walked to the door and opened it halfway.

"Everything is fine, Jack. Thanks for checking."

"No problem. Have a good night. Don't stay too late," the guard said, chuckling.

Dr. Emery shut and locked the door. He waited a few moments as the guard's footsteps disappeared down the hallway. "Sorry about that," he said.

"You know about the fossil?" Abi asked. "How is that possible?"

The professor smiled. "With a find like that, word spreads quickly, shall we say, to a select few."

This was disturbing. Up until now, the only ones who had any knowledge of the bone were Abi, Ethan, Ethan's dad, Joseph Nori, Shelly, Gen, Raymond—and the two men chasing Abi and the group.

"Do you have the bone?" the professor asked anxiously.

Abi slipped the sport bag from her shoulder and unzipped it. She carefully removed the bundled fossil, setting it on the table in front of them. As she began to unroll it, the professor's eyes widened. When he spoke, however, his voice, low key and unimpressive, did not give anything away.

"Yes, the femur from an allosaurus. And as we have heard, here is the interesting part."

"It's a spearhead . . ." Raymond exclaimed. "A spearhead that struck a live dinosaur."

The professor chuckled again. "I don't know about that."

"What do you mean?" Abi asked Emery. "What other explanation could there possibly be?"

"Interpreting the fossil record is always difficult. Since we were not present, much is speculation. The one fact we can be certain of is that a human could not have stuck a spear into a living allosaurus."

"I don't believe this," Ethan said. "Our lives have been threatened. My mom was almost killed. Why would anyone do that for nothing?"

"I wouldn't say that it is nothing," Emery said. "This fossil could be quite the conversation piece. Collectors may even value this bone as a curiosity. I assume these people chasing you wanted to make a quick buck. Lousy two-bit criminals. This happens frequently with unusual artifacts."

Ethan looked at Gen. To him, she appeared livid.

"But," Emery continued, "I do think I can help you. Leave the bone with me. Once those criminals realize you are not in possession of it, I'm certain they will leave you alone."

Abi looked at Ethan, then back at the bone. "Actually, I've grown rather fond of this old fossil, even if it is worthless."

"I understand," the professor said calmly. "But you've had a difficult few days. I believe I have bottled water in the kitchen. I'll be right back."

Dr. Emery quickly walked to the far end of the large room and disappeared behind a door. The four visitors looked uneasily at each other.

"What's going on, Mom?" Ethan said.

"I, I don't know. Maybe this really is nothing."

"He's lying!" Raymond said. "He knew about the bone before we got here, and he wants it for himself."

"He wouldn't do that," Ethan's mom said. "He's a scientist—not a thief."

Suddenly, Ethan motioned to Gen. On the table next to him was a phone with a light on; the first line, it appeared, was blinking. Just as Ethan started to reach for the receiver to listen, the light went out.

Moments later, Emery returned with four bottles of water. "Here you are. Just what the doctor ordered."

Ethan forced a small laugh. "Professor, I am amazed by the number of bones in this room."

"Ah, yes. I spend hours and hours categorizing and identifying them. However, you must understand most of the larger piles are not really bones."

"Not bones?"

"Let me show you."

The group followed the professor to a table piled with bones. "You see, they are actually plastic resin casts. When we rebuild a skeleton, we may only have five to ten percent of the actual bones. The rest are simulated."

Dr. Emery sorted through the pile in front of them. "Here we have the complete skeleton for an allosaurus, all in plastic resin. In fact, look at this femur. Hard to tell it from the real thing, isn't it?"

"I have a question," Ethan asked. "Who did you call just now?"

Emery flushed. "Call? I don't know what you mean."

"He used the phone, Mom. I'm sure he told someone that we are here."

"Is this true?" Abi looked hard at Dr. Emery.

Emery had no response. He slowly started backing toward the rear door.

"How could you?" Ethan's mom asked.

"You don't understand," Emery said. "Things are bigger than you and me . . . bigger than one unusual fossil. I have no choice in this matter."

"What about the *truth*? Isn't that what this is all supposed to be about?" Ethan's mom asked. "Your life's work has been all about searching and digging for the truth. This bone is truth, Dr. Emery. This bone could change things."

"That will never happen," the professor said. "It is not allowed."

Suddenly, footsteps could be heard running across the floor upstairs.

"Time to leave," Ethan said, motioning toward the back door.

Emery darted out the back door, slamming it shut and locking it from the outside moments before Ethan could turn the doorknob. The door was made of solid metal, with no window. Ethan looked but could not find a way to break it down. Since the professor's lab was below ground, the windows in the rest of the room were far off the floor.

"The hallway! *Now!*" Ethan shouted.

Ethan, Abi, and Raymond sprinted to the door and into the hallway. Ethan suddenly stopped. "Gen! Where's Gen?"

He dashed back into the bone room, where Gen was next to the table of bones, wrapping up the fossil and stuffing it into the sport bag. She quickly swung the straps over her shoulder and rushed to follow Ethan.

"I'm coming! I had to grab our fossil."

The four ran toward an exit sign flashing at the far end of the hallway. They had to avoid meeting whoever was rushing across the hallway upstairs.

Ethan pushed open the heavy door. A long cement stairway led up to street level. Just as quickly, a dark figure appeared at the top of the stairs.

"Found 'em. They're here!" he shouted.

"Back to the bone room," Ethan yelled. They sprinted to the large bone room. Someone else could be heard running down the opposite stairway. They shut and locked both doors.

"The tables!" Ethan yelled. All four got behind one of the tables and pushed it toward the door. When they got close enough they tipped it on its side, spilling the bones into a pile. Gray dust from the fake bones billowed into the air. They repeated this with the second table. Fake dinosaur bones were piled high along with the tables. The barricade was impressive, but the dust was thick in the air. Raymond started coughing.

"We don't have much time," Ethan said. He scanned the room again and noticed a large screen covering a ventilation shaft.

A loud bang against the door made Gen scream.

"Time for one of those brilliant ideas," Raymond managed to say between coughs.

"Here," Ethan said. "Help me push a table under that vent."

In seconds, the group shoved a third table some twenty feet, directly under the vent. Before jumping up on the table, Ethan grabbed a chisel and a hammer from a collection of tools. He was just high enough to reach the screen.

The crashing against the door grew louder. The glass window on the door shattered, and the barricade started to give way. Ethan nearly had the screen pried off. Another loud crash against the door caused the whole bone pile to shift. At the same time, with one final swing of the hammer, Ethan sent the screen crashing to the floor.

"Follow me," Ethan yelled as he jumped off the table. He led the group to a dark corner of the room, where they all ducked behind a small Dumpster.

One more crash, a few more curses, and the pile of bones and tables moved far enough for two men to burst into the bone room. One of them had a crew cut and cleared his throat loudly.

"Broderick, look there. The ventilation shaft. Go after them!"

"Me, Boss?"

"Yes, Broderick, you! Now! *Now!*"

Raymond fought to stifle a cough. He plugged his nose and closed his eyes tightly, forcing himself to remain quiet.

Both men climbed onto the table. The one called Broderick hoisted himself up to the vent and started crawling into the large ductwork.

"Hurry. No way to know how far they are. I'll go around to the back to see where this comes out."

Frost jumped off the table. Before he ran out of the room, he paused and scanned in every direction.

Raymond struggled with all his might to suppress the cough rising up in his throat. He couldn't last much longer before he would give away their position. Yet Whisper Man would not leave.

Ethan felt the man's eyes searching every part of the room. He knew the man was listening closely as well. The man with the icy voice finally cleared his throat and left the room for the hallway.

Raymond looked as though he were going to explode.

"Shh. Wait," Ethan whispered. They could still hear metallic thumps echoing from the vent. No sound came from the hall.

"OK, let's see if we can get out through the front door," Ethan said.

Raymond happily coughed, clearing his lungs of the gray dust.

"I'm proud of you, Raymond," Ethan said.

"Me?" Raymond said. "You're the one with the brilliant idea."

"Don't be too impressed. I saw it in a movie," Ethan said. He led the group carefully around their bone barricade to the door. Just as he stuck his head into the hallway, he stopped dead in his tracks. A large black pistol was inches away from his forehead.

Abi gasped. The man holding the gun cleared his throat. "Bravo on your efforts," he whispered. "Unfortunately for you, I watch movies too. But now, as you can see, it is time for you, your mom, and your little pals to stop this nonsense."

The four of them backed awkwardly into the dusty bone room. Frost motioned with his gun for them to move away from the door and stand against a table in the middle of the room.

"I am glad that all of you look frightened. You should be," Whisper Man said.

"Who are you? Why are you doing this?" Ethan's mom asked, frantically.

"One question at a time, Dr. Booker. My name is Frost. As to the second question, I find it rather amusing that you ask me about my motives. I will ask you instead. Why are *you* doing this? Why, Dr. Booker, do you lack the ability to comprehend the magnitude of this situation? Dangerous men have been chasing you, Dr. Booker. Yet you insist on running and dragging children along as you try to hide. Aren't there laws in this country?"

Raymond moved next to Gen and suddenly whispered, yet loud enough for everyone to hear.

"What about Ralph?"

Gen, still carrying the bag over her shoulder, immediately understood the ploy. She gave her brother a highly visible jab with her elbow. The man with the crew cut cleared his throat. "And where would Ralph be hiding?"

"No way I tell you, pal," Raymond said as he shifted his eyes a bit—as though he was unintentionally giving something away—toward the T. rex skeleton.

"Thank you, small one. You've been most helpful." Frost moved swiftly in the direction of the skeleton, but kept his pistol trained on Ethan.

"Get out here now, Ralph," he whispered. "The game is over." All was still except for the sounds of anxious breathing.

Frost grew irritated and cleared his throat in what sounded more like a growl. "I'll make this easy. I'll count to five, and if you're not out, I'll shoot one of your friends in the leg. That sounds more than fair. One . . ."

The man looked hard at the skeleton, trying to see anyone who might be hiding inside the mass of bones. Ethan quickly slid a bone off the table and held it behind his back.

"Two. This is not a joke, Ralph. Show yourself. Three." The man was right next to the skeleton now. Ethan gave Raymond a signal.

"Four!"

Raymond shouted, "Run for it, Ralph!"

The man glanced at Raymond and then frantically turned back, expecting to spot someone fleeing. Ethan took full advantage of the misdirection by throwing the bone hard. It was a perfect strike, taking out the left leg of the T. rex. The skeleton collapsed. The massive head landed directly on top of the man with the gun. Taking no chances, Ethan sprinted to the nearby table piled high with more bones. He dumped its entire contents on top of the already unconscious man, just for good measure.

Shouts and scrambling noises echoed from the vent. "Boss, are you all right? Boss! I'm coming!"

With no time to waste, all four raced past the bones, out the door, and back upstairs. Ethan pushed a large planter in front of the stairway door. Iron gates now separated them from the rest of the museum and the emergency exits. In the opposite direction, the front doors to the museum were chained shut. Two narrow windows of thick glass framed the door, one on each side. This would be their only exit. Ethan grabbed a heavy brass urn, charged, and flung it against the window. The urn bounced off. He tried a second time—with the same result.

Footsteps could be heard running up the stairs, followed by loud pounding against the door.

Ethan gave up on the window and turned his attention to the chains. Frantically, he hammered repeatedly at the chain and the lock.

"No good," he said. "I'll try the window again. Stand back." Ethan grabbed the urn tightly and backed up to get plenty of speed. He raised the urn over his head, let out a roar, and charged once again toward the window. Before Ethan could take three steps with the urn, however, the window shattered inward, into the museum. Fragments of glass flew inside, covering the foyer. One of the cement reptiles from outside came skidding across the tile floor, narrowly missing Ethan. Gen screamed loudly as all the alarms in the building went off. No one could move. No one understood what had happened. A shadowed figure peered in through the broken window.

"Run!" Ethan shouted, not really knowing where to run, but assuming whoever was coming in was after them. They all turned to follow him.

"Wait, it's me! Your dad!"

The scene had turned into utter chaos. The stairway door cracked loudly as the pounding increased, alarms were blaring, and out of nowhere, his dad had appeared.

Gen made the first move. "Come on, out through the window."

Mom and Raymond followed Gen through the narrow broken window. Ethan hesitated only for a moment before darting outside. And then he realized that his dad was not alone.

"Joseph!" Abi shrieked.

"Yes, it is me," Joseph said. "Did you think David could throw that cement lizard all by himself?" He grinned ever so slightly.

"I'm glad you're alive," Abi said.

"I'm glad we both are," Joseph said. "Although I am not sure how you could be alive. But there you are, just as your ex-husband predicted."

"The car is here," Ethan's dad said as the group ran down the sidewalk. His silver Buick was pulled up on the sidewalk right down the street from the museum entrance.

"Hurry. Jump in," Ethan's dad yelled.

They all climbed in, even though the last thing Ethan wanted was to be in his dad's car. However, he could see the yellow van across the street—sitting very low. Clearly, all four tires had been slashed. It was his dad's Buick or nothing.

The silver car sped away. No one emerged from the museum. Likely, no one was able to get a look at the car. Police sirens were approaching but were still a few blocks away.

Gen could tell that Ethan was distraught sitting in his father's car. She grabbed his hands and looked into his eyes.

"Ethan," she said, "We're safe for now. We have to trust him."

∞ ∞ ∞ ∞ ∞ ∞ ∞

Back in the museum, the man with the crew cut was talking on his phone.

"Yes, they were here, just as the professor said. Negative. We do not have the fossil. No, no, we did not miss them. They were here when we arrived."

He wiped his forehead with his sleeve, pausing in order to control his anger. "They were here. They escaped." He seemed to be strangling the words through his clenched teeth.

He listened for a long time and looked highly annoyed. "No, they are not professionals. I am surprised also. But now I am requesting additional resources. Of course, I am aware of what we have here—a teenage boy, his mother, a teenage girl, and her little brother. You don't need to remind me. But something is very different here. I can't explain it. This should have been easy. But we're three weeks later, and we're still at it . . . No, it's not because I'm getting old. It's something else at work that I don't understand . . . almost as if . . . no, nothing important. If you want this fossil, additional resources are gonna be needed . . . Yes, I would not hesitate to include those.

"I must remind you that time is growing short. In twenty-four hours, this fossil, of which you are so concerned, will be all over television. Everyone will know of it." Again he listened. His face reddened. "Likely, they're getting additional help. Yes, possibly her ex-husband, but I would not have suspected that. I am paid to anticipate such things. It is my job to know when it is warranted to request additional resources. I couldn't care less about your dinosaur bone, but if it so important to you, we need those resources—*now*."

CHAPTER TEN

*It might be going too far to say that the modern
scientific movement was tainted from its birth;
but I think it would be true to say that it was
born in an unhealthy neighbourhood . . .
Its triumphs may have been too rapid and
purchased at too high a price: reconsideration,
and something like repentance, may be required.*
—C. S. Lewis[7]

Ethan did not feel rescued. Running through the museum
with zero options of escape might have been better than
being trapped inside his father's car. *How did this happen? Why
are Dad and Joseph here? Why does Joseph appear to trust Dad?*

Ethan's mother sat in the front seat, with Joseph providing a buffer between her and David. Ethan could tell by her
body language that she was nearly panic-stricken. This was
understandable. She said she could trust Professor Emery.
She believed that his help was crucial, not just for the safety
of the fossil, but for the entire group. Now she was forced to
turn to a man she had no reason to trust. She looked nervously into the backseat before speaking.

"There are three children in the backseat, David. I have to know if we are safe."

"Yes, thank God. I'm not sure why Gen and Raymond are with you, but you're all safe now."

"You knew where we were . . ." Ethan said out loud, wondering how it was possible.

"Joseph had an inkling," Ethan's dad said. "He reasoned that your mom would have brought the fossil to Dr. Emery."

"A lucky guess," Joseph said. "First David worked hard to convince me that Dr. Booker was still alive. Now I am completely convinced."

"It's a miracle," David said. "I've been searching ever since I saw the front door of the house bashed in. Of course, I was horrified. I searched the house frantically, not knowing what I would find. Thankfully, the house was empty. I found no one lying in the rubble that was once your bedroom, Ethan. But why? To me it made no sense that someone would work that hard just to get to you, Ethan. No offense. I'm no genius, but I soon realized that your mom had to be alive. I also guessed that you escaped from the house and went to her. From there, I asked myself: Whom does she trust?"

"So you remembered Joseph," Abi said.

"I know it was years ago that he was your student. You would tell me stories of this Joseph Nori, of how hard he worked, of how proud you were of his character and desire to dig for the truth."

"You said that about me?" Joseph asked with genuine surprise and a bit of pride.

David continued. "I guessed that you wanted to show him the fossil. Who else would be able to share in the excitement of the discovery? Joseph was the logical choice. Joseph was also the only one who just might know where to find you."

"Yes," Joseph said. "You used to tell me about Dr. Emery. You consulted with him on occasion. You admired and respected him."

"Things change," Abigail said.

Ethan leaned forward. "Other things don't. Why did you agree to help my father, Joseph?" Everyone caught the bitterness in Ethan's tone. The car was quiet; no one spoke. The only sounds were the motor running and the cars passing by.

Joseph thought for a moment. "I listened to him, Ethan. I believe he loves you."

They drove quietly for a few miles, everyone processing the events of the last two days. David constantly checked his rearview mirror as he drove, but saw nothing suspicious behind them. Finally, Ethan broke the silence. "Dad, all of us are grateful to you and Joseph for getting us out of that museum, but I still find the whole thing hard to swallow. One day after you give Mom the fossil, she is attacked. Moments after she contacts me, our house is attacked. This Dr. Emery makes one phone call, and once again, we are running for our lives. Suddenly, out of the blue, you appear to save the day. You say you it was just a good guess. I'm not convinced that guessing was involved." Once again the car was silent. No one even tried to answer Ethan.

Watching only one lonely car go by, Ethan carried on. "Joseph says he trusts you. The problem is, Joseph does not know you as well as me and Mom. He doesn't know how many people you hurt just to get what you wanted. Here you are with your hands on a fossil that is apparently more valuable than I can imagine. This is a bad situation, and we're trapped here. You got us. For some reason that I don't understand, Joseph feels he can trust you. So does Gen. If you care at all about Mom or me, I need to hear the truth, Dad. Are you involved in any of this?"

Ethan's dad was quiet. He seemed to be choosing his words carefully.

"It's an easy question, Dad. Yes or no!"

"Of course not! No!" David was clearly irritated with Ethan's accusation.

"Right," Ethan scoffed. "Only four people knew about this stupid dinosaur bone—Mom, Aunt Shelly, Joseph, and you.

I trust Aunt Shelly completely. Mom only told Joseph. But somehow, some way, a bunch of other people still found out. A really bad bunch of people. Wasn't it enough just to divorce her?"

"What are you saying? Do you think I told someone about this?" Ethan's dad demanded angrily.

"Of course you did," Ethan said. "After you gave her the fossil, you realized its value and wanted it back. You must have called someone."

Ethan could see his father's knuckles turning white as he gripped the steering wheel tightly. A tiny bead of sweat ran down the back of his neck. No one in the car said a word, until Joseph spoke.

"It is quite possible that your father is telling the truth, Ethan. You see, I'm the one that told someone about the fossil. I made one phone call."

Ethan could not believe it. He slumped back into his seat, more confused than ever.

"Who did you talk to?" Abi asked Joseph.

"Technically, I didn't talk to anyone, per se."

"Joseph! *Who?*" she insisted.

"On the Internet I found a contact number for the National Science Foundation, the NSF. They are basically the top of the food chain as far as significant discoveries are concerned. Certainly, this is a significant fossil. No way did I want it to fall into the wrong hands. I was getting ready to leave the country, and I wanted to make sure this fossil received proper treatment." Joseph was shaking; he turned enough to look at Ethan face-to-face.

"You must realize I was not thinking of myself. I was thinking only of your mother, Dr. Booker. She deserves the best. The NSF must be one big organization. I never did talk to a real person. I navigated their automated system for a while, finally ending up in the Division of Paleontology. Once there, I still was unable to talk to a real person. I just left a message. Because of the importance of the bone, I left a very detailed message about the dinosaur fossil and the spearhead. I did not want to take any credit, so I mentioned that the person responsible was Dr. Booker. I figured they would be intrigued by my message and call back right away."

"Let me guess," Ethan said. "They never called."

"Never. Can you believe it?" Joseph said.

"Wait, wait," Raymond said. "Are you saying that the NSF is behind all this? That's ridiculous. The NSF sponsors *Mr. Wizard*."

"The NSF is just one group," Abi said. "Actually, many groups and organizations fund and oversee the entire scientific community. You've got the American Association for the Advancement of Science, the Board of International Science, the—"

"We get it, Mom. Let's just say many groups are out there," Ethan said.

"I'm sure many organizations exist that we don't even know about. They all work together, sharing everything," she added.

"So that's how Dr. Emery found out about the fossil?" Gen asked. "One phone call to an answering machine, and the 'select few' knew all about it."

"This is insane," Ethan said. "You're a scientist, Mom. Now you're saying that they're all evil."

"Science isn't evil," Gen said. "All science can do is reveal God's creation. Man is the one that gets off track."

"I shouldn't have called," Joseph said. "This is most certainly all my fault."

"None of this is your fault," Abi said. "In fact, you just rescued all of us from a museum. You and David," she added, looking around Joseph at her ex-husband.

The car drove on, into the darkness. No one spoke for miles. Exhaustion was taking its toll. Gen rested her head on Ethan's shoulder. That was totally sweet for Ethan. Raymond was leaning against his sister. They both were breathing slowly and deeply. Even Ethan's mom was tired enough that she was able to find some sleep, despite the fact that Joseph was snoring.

Ethan sat, wide awake, watching his father drive. Other than a couple of logging trucks and raccoons, the road was empty. Ethan didn't know what he felt. At one time he enjoyed all the anger deep in the pit of his stomach. The anger had been real and solid, and he knew exactly where he stood. Now that the rage was gone, he assumed he would feel lost. Instead, he felt something else that he did not expect. Something better than rage.

It was a glimmer of hope.

"Where are we going?" Ethan asked quietly.

"Somewhere. I don't know," David said. "Someplace where none of us have any connections or history. We have to make it difficult for anyone to find us. The sign back there said lodging was available in ten miles in a town I've never heard of. I guess we'll stop there. After a rest, we'll make a plan."

"Why did you leave?"

David took a deep breath. He looked at the sleeping woman who used to be his wife. "You deserve an honest answer, Ethan. And to be honest, I thought I wanted more. When I turned fifty, everything seemed to be going way too fast, like there was hardly any time left. I was scared. I'd always dreamed of doing these fun things, adventurous things. Perhaps I had even fantasized about them. When the business took off, I had all the money I needed to do whatever I wanted to do. For some reason, I wanted to be with a younger woman. I guess I figured my time was running out, and I didn't want to miss anything. I could tell you that I was too drunk to think straight. I was drunk a lot of the time. But I knew exactly what I was doing. I was a fool, Ethan. Come to find out, everything I really wanted, I left behind. I left you without a father for two years. I left your mom without a husband. I wish I could do it all over."

"That's not an option, is it, Dad?"

"No, it's not. I know that. I also know that consequences are real. Missing a baseball game is real. Loneliness and shame are real. I love you, Ethan, and I love your mom very much. More than anything, I would love a chance to be your dad again. Maybe someday, you can forgive me." He appeared to wipe tears from his eyes.

Ethan sat in silence. Gen squeezed his arm and smiled at him. Apparently, she wasn't asleep after all.

"I've spent the last two years being angry at you," Ethan said. "For most of those two years I was angry because you left. You hurt Mom. I could say it didn't affect me one way or the other, but I know that's a lie. I blamed you when she drove into the river."

Ethan paused. With all the complicated things that had happened, he was amazed how simple this moment felt. "But for being a fool? Yeah, someday, maybe I could forgive you for being a fool."

"Then, someday, you will make me very happy," David said.

"Then I suppose you might even have to forgive me for wrecking your bulldozer."

Abi's head shot around, her gaze fixed on Ethan. "Bulldozer?"

Gen leaned away from his shoulder. "You did that?"

"I knew it," Raymond said. Apparently he wasn't asleep either.

Ethan just shrugged. "Later, Mom."

They drove on, into the night.

CHAPTER ELEVEN

*From the moment a creature becomes aware
of God as God and of itself as self, the terrible
alternative of choosing God or self for the centre
is opened to it.*

—C. S. Lewis[8]

Ethan and his dad combined their cash to pay for the largest room in the small hotel. They could not chance using a credit card. Joseph and Raymond ran across the street to a convenience store to buy some food, also with cash. Joseph claimed to be a connoisseur of convenience-store food since he was an experienced bachelor. When they returned, heatedly debating something regarding Klingons, they delivered three liters of Mountain Dew, two boxes of Ritz crackers, and two cans of Cheez Whiz. Since Joseph had spied a microwave before leaving, they also bought a dozen pepperoni Hot Pockets.

The food and company were a brief but welcome relief from their predicament. For a time, Ethan was able to set aside the danger and narrow escapes from earlier in the day. His mother and father were sitting next to each other, having an actual conversation and smiling. Gen smiled as she happily zapped the Hot Pockets. They quickly deduced that three minutes and forty-four seconds was perfect. Ethan found the aroma strangely comforting, like sitting in his own kitchen on a Saturday night while his mother cooked frozen pizza for him and his friends.

Joseph and Raymond challenged each other to see who could sculpt the best allosaurus out of a glob of Cheez Whiz. Before long, a return trip to the store was required for additional sculpting supplies: two more jars of Cheez Whiz, plastic knives, and stir sticks. Obviously, the group needed to relax and recharge.

The television news carried a brief report about an incident at the Seattle Museum of Natural History. Professor Emery was interviewed. He stated that vandals had caused significant damage to some priceless collections and irreplaceable artifacts. Ethan couldn't help but be amused at the spin on the actual events. He presumed that Professor Emery's version of the truth would result in a large insurance check that would more than cover the "priceless" artifacts. Abi was especially annoyed at the TV report. However, the others convinced her that she should not waste any energy getting angry over Emery's lies, at least not tonight. Abi and the rest of the group soon returned to their conversations and their food.

Ethan didn't want to ruin the moment; however, this was as good a time as any to change the subject and maybe do some brainstorming. He thumped two empty Mountain Dew bottles together to get everyone's attention. "If anyone has a brilliant plan, let's hear it."

"What plan are you talking about?" Abi asked. "This is finished. I said very clearly, in English, that this ended with Dr. Emery. You agreed, Ethan. We never would have been in that museum today if you hadn't agreed that talking with Dr. Emery would be the final step. Only by some extraordinarily good fortune are we all still together and safe. This is bigger than we thought. We are done. Tomorrow morning we get back in the car and find the nearest police station. That is my brilliant plan, Ethan."

"Yes, you are absolutely right, Dr. Booker," Joseph said.

Ethan looked at Gen, his dad, Joseph, and Raymond. All four sat on the beds trying not to look at each other. They had just been through a traumatic day. Everyone was stressed, confused, weary, and ready to go home. But the thought of giving up the fossil bothered them all, especially his mom. No one wanted to make matters worse by saying anything that might upset Abi.

"Mom, you can't—"

"No, Ethan, I am not going to discuss this."

"Just listen to me for one minute."

"It's done, Ethan!" She turned to her ex-husband for support. "David, you tell him. He's your son."

Ethan's dad hesitated. He shuffled his feet and fiddled with a half-eaten cracker. "Abi, I truly want to support you. I mean, I *do* completely support you."

Ethan knew that his father did not want to put a wedge between himself and Abi.

"But, I think you should give your son a chance," David said very softly.

Abi's head and shoulders sagged. After a long silence, she reluctantly turned back and faced her son. "I'm listening," was all she could say.

"I know I promised," said Ethan. "I'm standing by that promise. I believe it does end with Dr. Emery. We're just not done with him yet."

"Yes, you are absolutely right, Ethan," Joseph agreed.

"Oh, for goodness sakes, Joseph," Abi groaned. "You can't agree with everyone!"

Joseph explained. "I simply changed my mind. Your son makes an excellent point regarding Dr. Emery. I do believe you deeply desire an additional confrontation."

Ethan watched his mother for a reaction. She slowly searched the faces of the people that surrounded her: Joseph,

Raymond, Gen, David, and Ethan. She looked at the green baseball bag that sat innocently enough on the small table in the corner—but in reality took over the entire room.

Ethan understood his mother well. He knew that she had no choice. More than anything she was a mom, but she was still a scientist. For her to walk away without ever finding out the answers would be difficult. She would always find it hard to sleep at night without really knowing who was responsible. No way could she guess who or what was behind all of this. Only one person had a direct connection to the answers: Dr. Emery. She had to see the man face-to-face, one more time.

Abi took a deep breath and stood up, looking at the Cheez Wiz creations on the side table. "Joseph, your allosaurus is proportionally the most exact. But Raymond wins because he has accurately depicted a meat-eater by having his dinosaur eat a small piece of pepperoni." Then she glanced at the green bag once more. "Like Ethan said, if anyone has a brilliant plan, let's hear it."

"I do," David said. "I'll be back in a second."

David quickly walked outside to his car. He returned with his arms full of maps. Because of his business, he always seemed to have detailed maps of the surrounding states. Dad always said how he preferred paper maps to a computer map. Paper maps provided a much bigger picture—a broader perspective in which to make better decisions. He spread them out on the floor of the hotel room.

He pointed to one of the maps. "This is where we are now. Does anyone know where Dr. Emery lives? Joseph? Abi? Any idea?"

"If I knew at one time, I don't remember now," Abi said.

"Not a problem," Raymond said. In no time at all, Raymond had asked permission to go to the hotel lobby, dragged Ethan with him, logged on to a computer with Internet access, and uncovered the doctor's home address, all without breaking a sweat. Not finding the address published in any directory,

Raymond had moved on to the university's listing of current staff. He had found both an office and home phone number, in case students needed to call.

A valid ID and password had been a little bit trickier. Not wasting time, Raymond had entered "Johnson" for an ID. After only four tries he had figured out the right password: "qwerty." Once he had obtained Dr. Emery's phone number, Raymond simply had to enter the digits into a search engine, yielding the address in .002 seconds.

"Perfect," David said, back in the hotel room. "That is right here." He motioned for Ethan to place his finger on the spot.

"Next, we need to predict where he might go tomorrow," David said.

"Tomorrow is Thursday. I can't say for sure, but Tuesdays and Thursdays are usually lecture days. My best guess is that he will be driving to the university . . . right here," Abi said, finding the location on the map.

David studied the map, then traced a route with his finger. "Based on those locations, this would be the most efficient route between home and school."

After studying the map a bit longer, David smiled, grabbed a pencil, and drew a big X on the map.

"Right there," he said. "Yes, that will do nicely. X marks the spot."

Everyone tried to peer at once at the X on the map, wondering why a place in the middle of nowhere was a good place.

"Don't worry," David said. "I'll explain in the morning. Now I need to make a phone call. I suppose the hotel phone is our safest bet."

Ethan's suspicions flared up again. "Who are you calling, Dad?"

"A friend of mine," David said, grinning. "Actually, a competitor who owes me a favor. Sometimes that's even better than a friend."

"I see," Ethan said suspiciously. "Calling another 'friend.'"

"Give me a chance, Ethan. Trust me. If you want to help your mom, trust me. You're welcome to listen in." He left the room to make his phone call from the hotel lobby. Ethan followed right behind him.

Ethan and his dad returned to the room shortly. "We're on for tomorrow," was all his father said. Ethan shrugged his shoulders. Although he no longer felt threatened by the phone call, he certainly did not understand the details.

"Sounds like we are in for a bit of a challenge tomorrow," Abi said. "We all better get some sleep."

The hotel was old and musty smelling. Still, the room was plenty big, and no one had to sleep in the bathtub. Everyone had a pillow and a soft place to lie down.

Ethan ended up on the couch. His feet dangled over the end, and one of the cushions felt like it had been stuffed with wadded-up newspapers. Fortunately, Ethan had countless things to take his mind off the couch. Not the least of which was that Joseph had joined the group. He was without a doubt the biggest nerd he had ever met, even bigger than Raymond. At the same time, Ethan liked him a lot and could easily see why he was his mom's favorite student.

And then there was Gen, who was as amazing as ever. It was crazy. At times Ethan had no idea what she was talking about, especially when she talked about God. Ethan desperately wanted to know what she knew and believe what she believed. He also really wanted to kiss her. Even though they were still in danger, Ethan constantly thought about how amazing that would be. For now it would have to wait, and, for that matter, Gen might have something to say about that.

On top of everything else, his dad was back. He had a plan for the morning, a plan to save the fossil. Maybe Ethan could trust him. Strangely enough, he did—or at least, he was tempted to. But seriously, how stupid could he be, Ethan wondered to himself. This was his totally untrustworthy, deadbeat dad. Still, earlier today, when his mom wanted to quit, his father had been on his side. He had supported him. That felt really good for a change.

Ethan's mind continued to spin from one thing to the next. He thought about his dad's plan and confronting Dr. Emery tomorrow. He wondered if the man with the crew cut would find them again. He wondered if they would be in a battle. If there was to be a battle, he was ready.

Exhaustion finally won the battle with the teenager's thoughts. Instead of envisioning tomorrow's encounter, he suddenly wished he were home playing baseball. Soon his thoughts became a vivid dream . . .

He stepped into the batter's box and signaled "time" to the umpire so he could dig his cleats into the dirt. The sunshine was warm on his face. A slight breeze was blowing the center field flag toward left field. He gripped his bat. The crowd behind him began chanting his name, "Ethan, Ethan." The pitcher leaned menacingly toward home plate, although Ethan could not see his eyes under the dark brim of his cap. Still, Ethan could feel his cold, hard stare. This simply made Ethan more determined. He did not care what pitch the catcher had signaled: curveball, slider, fastball: it did not matter. Ethan knew he would crush whatever pitch came his way. The ball flew toward the plate. To Ethan the baseball looked as big as a basketball. The crowd roared. Ethan gripped his bat hard and swung with all his strength. . . .

The scene changed. Ethan was no longer holding a bat. Now he was holding a spear. The sun still felt warm on his skin, but more than just his face. He realized he wasn't wearing much at all, except for something that covered him made from a material he did not recognize. The air smelled heavy with vegetation, but the sky was brilliant. High hills or mountains edged the horizon. Birds that he could not identify flew overhead. The ground felt hard and dry on his bare feet as he ran. He was moving quickly. He ducked under low-hanging tree branches and jumped over fallen limbs and jagged boulders. He was surprised how agile he was and how fast he could move across the rough terrain, as though he was made for this. The wind blew his long hair behind him. His legs moved powerfully and seemed to never tire. The spear felt good in his strong hands. He felt a fierceness that was hard to explain, as though he was afraid of nothing, that there was no battle he could not win. Never had he felt so strong, so brave, and so alive.

He was not alone. Others were running with him. They were dressed as he was, and they also carried spears. They were shouting, shrieking. Ethan shouted with them. They were a team, working together, or possibly fighting together. Somehow this place all made sense. He was meant for this, perfectly designed for this battle. But what were they fighting? He did not have to wait long for an answer.

The trees ahead of him exploded. Ethan was able to avoid the branches that landed all around him. The giant lizard, cut off by the thick forest and tired of running, would now turn and fight. The monster roared in anger. The others next to Ethan roared back and shook their spears menacingly. Ethan suddenly found himself in front of the group. He was the one chosen to take on the beast. He gripped his spear tightly and stepped slowly and purposefully from side to side, analyzing the best method of attack. The lizard was at least twice as tall as Ethan. Its head was enormous, made larger by the fact that its mouth was open, ready at any moment to tear apart each one of his attackers with his dagger-sharp teeth. The skin of the beast was a grayish brown, smooth and almost leathery—identical to the material that Ethan wore. The beast's massive chest heaved in and out, still breathing hard from the chase. Ethan continued to look for the best place to plunge his weapon.

The beast's dark eyes raged as he tracked the hunters' every move. Ethan knew that the beast would soon decide to attack. As deadly as the teeth were, Ethan first had to avoid its front arms. Even though they were short, they were incredibly strong. On the end of each of its arms were three long fingers with curved claws. They were perfectly designed for grabbing and holding prey. Once those claws sunk into Ethan's skin, escape would be impossible.

The others began chanting something that Ethan could not understand. They banged their spears on rocks and small trees. Ethan instinctively knew they were trying to distract the beast, to allow him, their lead hunter, the best chance of killing the monster. This was Ethan's moment. He sprang forward, directly toward the beast. The giant lizard roared and also sprang straight ahead. His fingers were spread out, ready to rip open the attacker with his claws. Ethan anticipated the lunge. He needed this advantage.

The only way to defeat the monster was to understand its natural instincts. The beast would always attack when cornered. Ethan dodged swiftly to the side, narrowly avoiding the claws. The giant lizard screamed in rage. Finding the exact spot where he could skewer the monster's heart with one deadly plunge, Ethan raised his spear without hesitation.

The beast was unbelievably quick. The claws did not grab him, but a sideways swipe knocked Ethan backward against a tree. Searing pain raced through his body. His hip and shoulder were on fire. His arm felt nothing and hung limp at his side. His spear was gone. The monster turned toward him and roared before lunging one last time. Before the beast could move, it screamed in pain and veered away. Ethan could see the shaft of a spear sticking out of the lizard's leg. Someone in his group had bravely saved him—for the moment. Dark blood dripped from the deep wound. The monster screamed again, brushed up against a large tree, and snapped off the shaft of the spear.

This would be his only opportunity. Ethan jumped to his feet and ran. Never before had he run as fast. He felt like he was *flying. Even so, when he looked behind, the monster was gaining, his claws clicking together, his dark eyes turning red, completely enraged. Ethan jumped a huge boulder with a single leap, but found himself high up on the edge of a cliff. Below him was nothing but an endless abyss. The beast flew at him. Ethan could see the claws ready to sink into his skin. He could feel his hot breath. Jumping was his only option. He screamed out loud as he fell. The sky spun above him. He tumbled into the abyss, down, down . . .*

"Ethan, wake up. Ethan."

As he opened his eyes, Gen was leaning over him rubbing his shoulder. For a moment he had no idea where he was.

"You were having quite a dream," she explained softly. "I'm right here. Everything's all right."

Ethan looked around the large hotel room. Now he remembered. Everyone else appeared to still be sleeping. He realized that he was drenched.

"Was it a fun dream, or a very bad one?" Gen whispered as she reached for a glass of water from the table.

Ethan took a long, thirsty drink. "It was both. I was in a battle with a dinosaur."

"Who won?"

"Not the dude all covered in sweat," Ethan said.

"I guess that's what happens when you fill up on junk food before going to sleep," Gen said with a smile. She slowly leaned over and gently kissed him on the forehead. "I hope that makes it better."

"It's a start," Ethan said as he pulled her closer and kissed her on the lips. It was not a long kiss, but it was the first. "Yeah, that is better," Ethan said softly with a smile.

Gen smiled back and squeezed his hand. "If you need anything, I'll be right over there." She took a small step away, then spun back around and returned for another kiss. Then, without saying a word, she got up and returned to her rollaway bed.

Ethan went to the bathroom to towel off and splash some water on his face before he lay back on the couch. He had no doubt that there was going to be a battle tomorrow. Hopefully the outcome would be different than his dream. He looked at Gen. They just had their first and second kiss. Sleep would definitely be difficult for the rest of the night.

CHAPTER TWELVE

The Bible is one of the greatest blessings bestowed by God on the children of men. It has God for its author, salvation for its end, and truth without any mixture for its matter. It is all pure.
—John Locke[9]

Morning arrived far too early. Ethan may have been the first one awake, but Joseph was the first one out of bed. He made a fresh pot of coffee before leaving. He soon returned with Pop Tarts. Hotel coffee and Pop Tarts was certainly not a feast, but hopefully it would be sufficient for the day ahead. Joseph stated proudly that he had aced many a college test fortified with just such a breakfast.

Gen told Ethan that she needed to contact her parents, who were still out of town. They decided the safest bet was sending an email from her account, using the hotel computer. In her email she wrote that she was bored but everything was fine . . . and that Raymond was being lazy and had only sold four popcorn balls.

"I don't want them to worry," she said. "But it's difficult to not be completely honest with them."

Ethan groaned. "Stop it. You know you can't tell them what's going on. That could endanger all of us *and* the fossil. Besides, you really didn't lie."

"Oh yes, I did. I said I was bored. Look, they already sent a response. They say, 'We are sorry that you are so bored. Maybe you should call that nice Ethan boy and see if he's doing all right.'"

"Talk about bad advice," Ethan said.

"Hurry and eat," David ordered the group. "We need to be on the road in twenty minutes."

"Dad, can you tell us the details?" Ethan asked. "I only got an overview last night."

The basic plan was simple. Get Dr. Emery away from the university, the museum, his home, any place where he would be able to contact someone quickly. He had to be contained, quickly and discretely. In order to have any time to question him, they could not allow him to make a phone call; they would have to secure his cell phone quickly to make this plan work.

The specifics of the plan were much more involved. David's phone call the night before was to a competitor named Scott Corvallis, owner of the Corvallis Heavy Equipment Company. As luck would have it, Scott was in charge of a major road construction project within ten miles of the X on David's map. Scott Corvallis was happy for the opportunity to pay back a favor. No questions were asked, but Mr. Corvallis commented that someone must owe David a lot of money. The Corvallis Heavy Equipment Company would provide David with everything he needed, including one steamroller, one bulldozer, a few signs, and one uniform.

"Scott also said he is happy that we are back together," David said, looking at Abi.

"Together!" Abi exclaimed, her face suddenly red. "That is a discussion for later," she said firmly, after regaining her composure.

"You're right. I'm sorry," David said.

Ethan assumed that his mother actually did want to have that discussion later. His father appeared to be remorseful about his midlife crisis. Perhaps his mother would be able to forgive him. That was most likely a difficult thing to discuss right now, while their lives were still in danger.

"You've got a lot of nerve, David," she said through tight lips.

"I know," he said. "We might just need some of that today. All right, everyone in the car. I'll explain more details of the plan along the way."

They drove for a couple of minutes, heading for the X on the map. "We are going to utilize what we refer to in the business as the off-road-squeeze," David said.

"Scott Corvallis is delivering the equipment we need on two flatbed trucks. Ethan, I know that you are somewhat familiar with the cab of a big machine. Now you get to officially learn how to drive one."

∞ ∞ ∞ ∞ ∞ ∞ ∞

Scott Corvallis was waiting for them. The bulldozer and steamroller were already off the flatbeds and running. Scott offered to drive the bulldozer. David thanked him, but said that his son was very capable.

"That's great to have your family involved with the business," Corvallis said. "I envy you. I have two kids, and neither of them has any interest at all."

"You never know," David said. "Things change."

Scott wished David good luck and drove off. In a matter of minutes, everything was in place.

David gave Ethan a quick lesson on the bulldozer. All he had to do was drive and steer. He had no need to learn how to operate any of the other controls. Driving and steering were enough. Ethan couldn't help the strange sense of irony. Here he was, sitting in the cab of a bulldozer that he was going to drive for his father. Only three days ago he was trying to destroy one of his father's bulldozers. He had to admit, this was better.

Everything was set. Abi, Raymond, and Joseph were waiting in the car, concealed in the trees. They were positioned a quarter of a mile ahead of Ethan and Gen. Gen was the only one that got to wear a disguise. Her assignment for the trap was to play the part of a road construction worker. Corvallis had provided a fluorescent orange vest, a yellow hard hat, large reflective sunglasses, and a walkie-talkie to complete the look. Gen stood off on the side of the road behind a large barrier—also provided for them.

The picturesque stretch of road had very little traffic. Chances were good that Emery was, in fact, driving to the university today. To make sure he wouldn't change his usual schedule, a call was placed to Emery early in the morning, explaining that the bone room at the museum would be closed all day so the insurance investigators could complete a thorough inspection of the damage. David was the one who had actually made the phone call, but Emery had no reason to doubt its authenticity. Since there was no reason for him to go to the museum, Gen and Ethan expected him to drive by soon. For now, all they could do was wait.

Ethan didn't mind. He was excited. His father's plan was a good one. Besides, Gen looked great in her hard hat and shades. Quickly, she raised the walkie-talkie to her ear. That must have been the signal from Abi. She waited for one more car to pass, and then she put all her strength into the heavy barrier. Half lifting, half dragging, she moved it across the road just in time. A bright white Range Rover pulled up to the barrier and stopped. Ethan could not see the driver, but assumed it was Dr. Emery on his way to the university.

Gen walked to the driver's window. Ethan couldn't hear the conversation, but earlier, when they rehearsed, he had played the part of Dr. Emery.

"Road's closed ahead," Gen would say. She was to speak in incomplete sentences and be a bit rude.

"But I need to get to the university," Ethan had said in a deep, dignified voice.

"Road's closed. Gas line. You'll have to take the detour." She would then point to a very narrow dirt road, perpendicular to the main road.

"Surely, there must be another way."

"Look, Mac"—Mac had been Ethan's suggestion—"you could turn around and hop on Highway 23, but that'll take you about forty minutes. This road here will just take ya ten."

Now all of this was happening in real time. Watching, Ethan knew that Emery was looking at the small dirt road to his left.

"It looks rough," Emery said, a slightly wrinkled look of worry on his face, to the young construction worker just outside his vehicle window.

"Come on," Gen said, looking over Emery's Range Rover. "This is a big ol' four-by-four. Lemme guess: you don't want it to get scratched."

The strategy was working just like they planned. Emery turned the wheel and started down the dirt road. Gen waited until he was out of sight and then dragged the barrier all the way off the highway. Ethan started up the bulldozer and waited for Gen to climb on board.

"That was fun," she said, throwing her vest and hard hat behind the seat.

Ethan gave her a big hug. "Nice work. Did you use the 'Mac'?"

"Of course. I felt very powerful. I might have to rethink my idea about becoming a molecular biologist."

Ethan headed down the dirt road after Dr. Emery. Abi, Raymond, and Joseph were right behind them in the car. He couldn't go very fast, but it didn't matter. The trap was set. The off-road-squeeze had been set in motion.

Already, Emery would be noticing that the dirt road was closing in on him. Soon the path would shrink to a single car width. At the end of the narrow portion, David would be waiting for him perched on top of a massive steamroller. In fact, Emery should be seeing the steamroller right about now.

This assumption was verified as a large column of steam rose into the air above the trees. That indicated that the steamroller was running and coming back toward Ethan.

Anytime now, Emery should reappear, driving in reverse.

"There he is," Gen said. "I bet he is not too happy."

Ethan blared his horn loudly at the Range Rover as he rumbled forward. At this point, Ethan was certain that Emery was frantic. He stopped his car and shifted back into forward. Any amount of forward motion was short-lived as the steamroller was nearly upon him. The Range Rover stopped right there, but Ethan continued ahead. The sound of the large metal blade against the rear of Emery's four-by-four was especially satisfying. Ethan laughed when the professor's brake lights appeared. The bulldozer moved ahead so smoothly that Ethan couldn't tell if the huge machine was actually pushing anything or not. Ethan continued pushing the expensive Range Rover—directly into the steamroller.

Even with the noise of the big machines, Ethan could hear Dr. Emery screaming. With the professor pressed between them, Ethan and David stopped advancing, but kept the big machines running. The panicked professor reached for his phone. Gen was already out of the cab. She reached in the window and snatched the phone, flinging it far into the woods where it would never be found. Emery was completely trapped and now totally helpless. Suddenly he did not appear to be the same self-confident, dignified man they had first encountered in the museum.

Abi, Ethan, Raymond, Joseph, and David joined Gen at the side of Dr. Emery's Range Rover. He looked sick. Abi walked directly up to the window, trying very hard to control her emotions.

"Dr. Emery," she said, "you will now tell us the truth."

CHAPTER THIRTEEN

The truth which has made us free will in the end make us glad also.

—Felix Adler[10]

Emery looked around and considered his captors. Unbelievably, the professor had regained his composure, once again displaying a misplaced air of authority. He tapped his fingers on his steering wheel. "There's nothing I can do for you."

Ethan nodded toward his dad. David climbed back up into the steamroller and shifted it into drive. Ethan could see beads of perspiration forming on the professor's bald head. The huge steamroller rumbled forward, snapping off the front bumper and popping the headlights, but still moving ahead. The professor was horrified.

"You must be crazy!" he screamed.

The roller squeezed the front of the Range Rover toward the ground. Steam rose into the air from the fractured radiator. The buckling frame made all sorts of bizarre noises. Suddenly the hood popped off, flying straight back into the windshield. The glass cracked loudly.

Dr. Emery screamed again and tried to escape out the passenger door. The frame was so badly bent, the door wouldn't budge. When the airbag exploded, Dr. Emery was knocked hard against his seat, his glasses sailing toward the rear of the Range Rover.

"Stop. *Stop!* I'll tell you anything you want to know!"

Ethan signaled to his dad, and the steamroller stopped. Dr. Emery was completely out of breath. Speaking was hard for him.

"Answers?" he gasped. "Please, get me out of here first."

"Not yet," Ethan said.

The professor knew he had absolutely no bargaining power. "Sure, I have plenty of answers. Not that they will do you any good."

"The fossil is real, isn't it?" Abi asked.

"It very well may be," gasped the professor, mopping his forehead with his tie.

"You wanted it for yourself, didn't you?" Ethan said. "You wanted the money."

The professor started to laugh but ended up merely coughing. "That is probably the last thing in the world I would want. People are so narrow-minded. I don't know why I am even trying to explain. None of you can possibly comprehend the big picture here. As I told you earlier, this is bigger than any one fossil."

"How big?" Abi asked.

Emery sighed. "Once the NSF caught wind of your discovery"—he nodded in Joseph's direction—"thanks to Joseph here, all of the major players were notified, from the science heads of the major universities to Pugwash."

"Pugwash? What's a *Pugwash*?" Ethan asked.

"Dr. Booker, I believe you are familiar with the group. Perhaps you can enlighten your entourage while I catch my breath."

Abi looked troubled, but explained. "Pugwash is a powerful scientific organization, consisting of highly placed government officials and highly respected scientists, some of whom are Nobel Prize winners. They met initially in 1957 in Pugwash, Nova Scotia, following a proposal by a couple of upstarts. Albert Einstein to name one."

"Very good, Dr. Booker. Now if you please, explain to everyone why they met. Was it to ban religion? Was it to figure out how to steal fossils? Tell them, Dr. Booker."

"They met in order to save the world from nuclear disaster."

"To save the world," Dr. Emery repeated. "That's right, some of the greatest minds on the planet trying to save us all, back in 1957. Pugwash is more powerful than ever, and they are still concerned with saving the world. The NSA and the US State Department know about the fossil, too. In matters of such grave importance, government agencies all work together. They share information."

No one moved. No one could speak. This new perspective was more confusing than ever.

"What did I say?" the professor said. He tried again to open the driver's side door, but the once shiny Road Ranger was completely bent. "You just did not know what you were dealing with. I was not lying when I said you should give me the bone. You would have been much safer."

"The NSA? The US State Department?" Gen questioned. "Why?"

"Were you not listening when I said this was bigger than you could imagine? This is futile. I have nothing else to say," Emery said.

Just then, a puff of smoke spewed from the crushed engine compartment. The smoke thickened until it burst into a small flame. David rushed back to the steamroller, where he pulled out a bright red fire extinguisher. He pointed the nozzle at the flame, and then looked at Dr. Emery.

"Well, put it out!" screamed the frantic professor, once more clawing at the door.

"I will," Ethan's dad said calmly. "But, you were just telling us about the NSA and the State Department."

Dr. Emery had no way to know how far David would take this. He decided it would be best to talk fast.

"Fine. Do you not understand the role of the State Department in our government? You can read it in their mission statement, which says, 'To protect national interests, security, and promote a prosperous world.'" Emery raised his fingers to make little quotation marks in the limited space above the steering wheel. "The US State Department is committed to working with institutions of higher learning, leveraging resources in order to do all those things. Do you have any idea the amount of resources available between our government and our universities? Do you have any comprehension of their combined power and reach? Granted, we underestimated the amount of resources required to retrieve your fossil."

Emery pounded on the steering wheel a little harder with each admonition. "Now put that fire out!"

David sprayed a small puff onto the growing fire. The flames went out, but dark smoke rose into the air as the fire continued to smolder.

"It's not completely out," Emery shrieked. "It may start again."

David peered around the hood. "I believe you are correct."

Joseph took a turn at the caged defendant. "So, you are admitting that you are a part of this entire operation."

"Of course," the professor said. "I work hard to keep our nation prosperous and safe."

"OK, I'll admit," said Raymond, walking up closer to the front of the Rover, "I'm narrow-minded and shortsighted. So explain to us how our fossil has any connection to the government or Pugwash or anything."

Ethan was quick to add, "And if your answer doesn't make sense, I'm sure Dad would be more than happy to start up the steamroller again."

Dr. Emery looked nervously through the cracked windshield at David, then back to Abi. There was no need to worry about the steamroller as the engine fire erupted once again. "It's burning again! Hurry, put it out!"

David pointed the extinguisher at the engine, but simply looked at the professor. "Seems to me you were explaining about some connection to the government."

"This is unbelievable!" The professor was nearly sobbing. "I will tell you everything. Please, Mr. Booker."

David looked at Abi. She nodded, suggesting that David show a bit of mercy. He sprayed the fire once again, still letting it smolder just enough that a thin line of black smoke curled out of the mangled hood.

"Thank you," Emery said, nervously looking at the smoke. "Now you must listen to me. Dr. Booker, you were planning on presenting that fossil on a large and visible stage. Were you not?"

"Of course. This fossil is an incredible discovery that will topple current theories."

"That would have been a terrible mistake. One that would never have been allowed."

"And why is that?" Gen asked, stepping forward to stand by Ethan.

Dr. Emery was running his fingers through his hair. He seemed frustrated that the small group encircling his smashed-up Range Rover could not understand the immensity of the situation. "What is it that you are most willing to give up? Your security? Your peace? Your prosperity?" he asked, noticeably anxious to get out of his wrecked vehicle.

"I enjoy all of those things. I also enjoy truth," Abi said.

"Truth? What is truth?" Dr. Emery pushed with all his weight against the door again. "Let me out of here, I beg of you."

Ethan looked at Gen, then back at Emery. "Not until you finish. You said you would tell us everything. Tell us about truth."

With a sigh of surrender, Dr. Emery leaned forward and started to explain. "Let's narrow this down. Which is the greater good, truth or prosperity? I am all for truth. But without prosperity, we are lost. You are correct, Ethan, when you say that the money is important. To be more precise, the economy is the most important. Do you know the greatest thing that ever happened to our economy? The computer? The automobile? None of those, I'm afraid.

"The greatest thing that happened to our economy was the theory of evolution. Creation without God is putting man in the center. After years of compelling our universities to be enlightened and controlling the debate in our schools, society finally accepted the inevitable. World productivity, especially America's productivity, has exploded. So speaking of God, thank God for evolution. Evolution completely removed God from our very existence. Without God, the floodgates were opened. We now have a nation committed to individualism and materialism. A nation where self-gratification has no limits." With a final flurry, Dr. Emery stuck his head out the Rover's window as far as he could, his eyes burning with righteousness. "We now have a strong nation. A prosperous nation."

Raymond was the one to finally break the spell. "But . . . most people believe in God. It's even on our money: 'In God We Trust.'"

"People don't care if the word God is printed on their money. They care more about what they can get with that money. I suppose people can trust Him on their money, but still doubt His existence," Emery said, calming down a bit. "Evolution nurtured and cultivated that doubt. Our economy does much better when people do not believe in God. All of that 'where your riches are, so lies your heart,' and 'camel through the eye of the needle' stuff can destroy an economy.

Why, someone might think they really don't need that new car or that bigger house or that giant screen TV. If thinking like that caught on, the stock market would crash. Think about your retirement funds."

"You're wrong, Dr. Emery. I know lots of people who go to church," Raymond said.

"Good for you, young man. I go to church, too. I read the Bible. It really is an interesting piece of literature. But you see, believing in God and going to church are two different things. Some people go to church simply to get rid of their guilt and feel better about themselves. Most simply like to be a part of a club, a place of belonging, where they can wear their new outfits and show off their new car. By Monday morning they've forgotten about God and are happily buying designer jeans, Botox treatments, and five-dollar cups of coffee.

"People don't actually believe what they hear in church. They believe in science. Creation of our world, without a creator, without God, is science. People would rather be intelligent than blindly persist in believing words that were written in a book thousands of years ago. Intelligent people simply will not argue with scientific facts. Millions of years, evolution. That kind of science is wonderful. People forget that creation through evolution is a theory. They see it as an indisputable fact. This is a wonderful thing. Now people don't need God. They don't pursue contentment. What they want is gratification. Our economy thrives."

Dr. Emery relaxed into the driver's seat. He appeared pleased that those standing around his crumpled Range Rover were uneasy with what he had just told them. Then, sitting up alert again, he continued. "Dr. Booker, do you know what your problem is? Perhaps you yourself think you are God. You think that you will stab at the foundations of our prosperity? Good heavens, Dr. Booker, our entire economy would collapse. Please, do not worry. That will never happen. That fossil, Dr. Booker, poses a bigger threat to national security than any terrorist with a dirty bomb. They thought this situation could be handled quickly and simply. They were wrong. But believe me, it will be handled. Science, as usual, will save us."

CHAPTER FOURTEEN

There are two ways to be fooled. One is to believe what isn't true; the other is to refuse to believe what is true.

—Soren Kierkegaard[11]

Gen climbed back into the cab to hitch a ride. Abi, Joseph, and Raymond were already in the Buick, backing up all the way to the road. David made his own path around Dr. Emery through the woods—accidently knocking a few small trees on top of the Range Rover, where Dr. Emery was mercifully left to fend for himself. David had put the engine fire completely out, and briefly considered duct taping Emery's wrists to his steering wheel to keep him from escaping anytime soon. Abi cautioned David that their actions toward Emery, however justified, were already bordering on criminal. Duct taping would most likely verge on kidnapping.

Ethan struggled to control the huge machine as he backed down the narrow dirt road. The exhaustion of the past few days had suddenly overtaken him. His vision blurred as he strained to keep his eyelids open. A few moments earlier he was energized, fighting the good fight. Now he felt overwhelmed and defeated. The words of Dr. Emery echoed in his head: "terrorist," "threat to national security," "stabbing at the foundations of our prosperity . . ."

Ethan glanced quickly at Gen. She smiled back at him. Gen's insistence that he was "meant to be here" seemed absurd to say the least. Perhaps she thought this attitude would calm him. Instead, it made Ethan angry. The safety of the entire group was more at risk than ever, yet she was looking perfectly at ease. Ethan thought briefly about confronting her, but changed his mind.

Gen would tell him that God is in charge. She would maintain that all things happen for a reason. That made no sense. What was the reason for his mother driving off the bridge? How did it do him any good to believe she was dead? What was the purpose of having to protect the fossil and being chased only to find out that they were now considered threats to the United States? If God was behind this, if He intended for the fossil to be uncovered, if He intended to send a bolt of truth into a world bent on turning away from Him, this was a peculiar way of doing it.

Soon all their troubles, all their efforts, would be for nothing. Ethan could see no other outcome than for this to end badly. At least now Ethan understood. His mother was dangerous. They all were dangerous. Their knowledge and their unusual possession constituted a legitimate threat to a particular world order that was promoted, rewarded, and defended by those who benefited most. The truth revealed in the fossil had the power to create real change, where change was not allowed. Their battle was against an entity that was large, pervasive, and had no time for the truth.

Even though Ethan was driving a machine weighing more than thirty tons, he felt powerless. The beast he was fighting was much bigger. The NSA, the US State Department, and whoever this Pugwash was . . . they were all beyond his control. This was crazy! How could they be in the middle of something this big? Still, someone must be scared. At least that bit of knowledge made Ethan feel better. Emery certainly had been bluffing back at the museum when he understated the significance of the fossil. Properly handled and presented to the world, this bone with a spearhead stuck in it would forever damage the status quo.

But this all depended on the fossil, and they would soon lose it. The battle was familiar. Years earlier a small band of humans fought against a mighty creature. All they had for weapons were spears. The beast was massive, yet the savages fought because their lives depended on it. The result of that battle would be repeated. Once again a small band of humans underestimated the power of the behemoth. The head of the spear would injure, but not destroy. Once again, they would fail. All had been for nothing.

The bulldozer and steamroller eventually made it back to the road. Ethan and his dad parked them next to the barricade, where they would be recovered the next day. Ethan, Gen, and David joined the others waiting by the Buick. Gen reached into the car, grabbed the green bag, and slung it over her shoulder. Abi looked at the bag—then stood firm and resolute. "We're going to give them the fossil. It's the only chance we have."

Raymond nodded.

"Agreed," Joseph said. "According to Dr. Emery, we have no choice."

"We probably don't have long for them to find us," Ethan said. He took out his cell phone. The number for the man with the crew cut was saved in his recent history. "I'm going to call them. If we surrender, they might just take the bone and leave us all alone. Any objections?" Ethan looked at each one standing around the car.

"Yes. I object," David said.

"Go right ahead and object," Abi said. "Ethan, make the call." Ethan hesitated. Once again, he was forced to choose between his mother and his father.

Joseph cast his vote. "Your mom is right, Ethan," he said. "This is out of our control. I agree that our best option is to give them the fossil. They may let us be. Who knows what may be heading our way right now. The government is very good at finding people. Maybe drones are tracking us right at this moment."

"Cool," Raymond said, looking up into the sky.

"Just let me make one phone call first," David suggested. "Ethan, could you reach my phone in the glove box?"

Ethan retrieved the phone but held it tight. He looked at his mother. Slightly more than three weeks ago, her car had been slammed from behind and launched off a bridge. By some miracle she had survived. Since then she had been attacked more than once, her family threatened, and her spirit nearly crushed. The fossil was no longer worth it to her. She was done.

He looked at his dad, and Ethan's emotions welled up, messing with his mind, removing any chance of thinking clearly. This man had abandoned him when he was fifteen. What kind of man would do that? This man had left his wife for some woman he met in a bar. That kind of a man did not deserve to be called a father. Yet, here he was—helping them, supporting them. Was this a game? Was his father challenging his mother out of spite, or was he stepping up and leading? Ethan had no clue what was motivating his dad; still, Ethan acknowledged to himself that he was pleased his father was here when he was truly needed. None of this made any sense. The only thing Ethan was sure of was his confusion.

Only one person could make this decision.

"Gen?" he asked. "What's our next step?"

Gen smiled at Ethan. "There is a reason we are all right here, right now," she said. "After everything your mom has been through. After everything that Joseph and the rest of us have been through. There is a reason that your dad is back after two years. Let him make the call."

Ethan glanced at his mother, who looked utterly defeated, and then quickly handed the phone to his father. David thought for a moment, and then dialed a number.

"Just curious. Who are you calling, Dad?" Ethan said.

"Mr. J. Sterner," his dad answered. "He owes me a favor."

The group looked at each other, slightly confused.

David reached a secretary. "Yes, Mr. Sterner, please. It is about his pond." David knew that would put him right through.

"You mean J. Sterner, the head of Sterner broadcasting?" Abi asked.

"Yes, that's the one," David said as he held for a moment. After a few moments of David holding and everyone else looking at one another, a man came on the line. "Mr. Sterner, this is David Booker . . . No, no, your pond will be just fine . . . Yes, you are very welcome. About that, I was wondering if you could do me a favor . . . When? Well, right at this very moment . . . No, actually, I am not kidding, Mr. Sterner."

Ethan slowly caught on. His dad's phone call was perfect. Sterner Broadcasting was the biggest cable news network in the Northwest. Full media coverage might just be the best way to protect them and the fossil. Ethan was once again proud of his father, at least for the moment.

"Here's the best part, Mr. Sterner. This could be one of the biggest stories ever for your broadcasting company. If you do this, your company will have exclusive rights . . . Yes, I am being serious, very serious . . . No, I cannot give you details over the phone . . . Sorry, I won't be able to come to your studios."

David looked at his ex-wife. "No, I haven't been drinking. Look, Mr. Sterner, I need you to send a helicopter, camera crew, and your best investigative reporter right now."

He paused to listen. "Well, in two hours your crew might be too late . . . Yes, I'm sure this will cost you a lot of money, but, as you said yourself, you do owe me. If your crew gets here in time, the story will be well worth your investment."

Ethan was intrigued. Coverage by the Sterner Broadcasting Company was exactly what they needed. His dad's phone call was well played.

David looked at the cell phone, fully realizing the consequences. "I must tell you, Mr. Sterner, a competitor will try to get to this story before you . . . Yes, I'm pretty sure they are on their way now . . . No, no. I would much prefer that you got the story before them. The problem is, if they get here before you, there will *be* no story . . .Well, that is the chance you will have to take."

David was right to assume that the man with the crew cut, and perhaps many others, knew their location. After all, they were considered a real and credible threat to the government. At the very least, David's cell phone would have been traced. The fossil and its little entourage were sitting ducks.

"We are on Highway 92 and County Road 4 . . . Yes, in Becker County. I assume your nearest news helicopter is in Seattle. We will start driving toward you in an effort to meet up as quickly as possible. For reasons I cannot explain right now, I am unable to give you a description of my car. Don't worry. When we see your helicopter, we will become as visible as possible . . . Actually, yes, I am expecting a bit of trouble . . . No, unfortunately, I cannot tell you any more. Get that bird in the air, Mr. Sterner. Now! Please!" David hit "end" on the call.

"Now, all we have to do is play keep-away from the guys in the black cars until the news crew gets here," he announced to the others.

"That really was J. Sterner, of Sterner Broadcasting?" Abi marveled. David nodded.

Her mood brightened. "What are we waiting for? Let's go!"

"Everyone in the car," David said. "We have an appointment with Sterner Broadcasting Company somewhere between here and Seattle."

"This is so cool," Raymond said. "Once we get on TV with the fossil, those bad guys can't touch us."

"That's what we're hoping for," David said.

"You know, Raymond, if you get on TV, your friends and your parents will probably see you," Ethan said while scrambling into the backseat of his dad's car once again.

"How cool is that?" Raymond said, waiting for his sister to slide to the middle. "Hold on, you said 'parents'? Oooh, I'll be so grounded. Wait a minute. I'll be fine. I'm not the babysitter. Gen's the one who will be grounded—probably for life. Worst babysitter ever." He bumped her shoulder as he quickly slid in beside her.

"I think this is a good plan, Mr. Booker," Joseph said. "Everything rests upon the fossil. The guys who are chasing us only want the fossil. Like Professor Emery said, no one will believe anything that we say anyway. The fossil will speak the loudest."

"You're right, Joseph," Gen said. "We have to pray that the news crew can find us first."

Highway 92 was a moderately traveled two-lane road. Any commuters who might live this far out were already at work. Traffic was light by late morning. The silver Buick was among a scattered line of vehicles, all headed for Seattle. David was obviously in no hurry to pass. He wanted to keep moving along with the traffic and draw no attention to their vehicle.

"When the fossil gets on TV, everyone will understand the truth. That will be awesome," Raymond said. "Things are really going to change. The things they teach us in school will change. The way we look at our world will change. Just think. People will start looking at their Bibles differently. Maybe they will actually believe what it says, cover to cover. Heck, we might have to show up early to church just to get a seat."

"Maybe," Gen said.

"What do you mean by that?" Raymond asked. "We have proof now, right in that green baseball bag."

"I agree with you," Gen said. "The thing is we already have proof. Proof is all around us. Look at these incredible mountains, streams, trees. Think about how the sun is the perfect distance from the earth to keep it just the right temperature. Remember, the Bible says, 'Since creation His attributes are clearly seen . . . we are without excuse.'"

Joseph picked up on the conversation. "I think Darwin had an excuse."

"What?" Ethan said.

"Well, he had this rudimentary microscope. To see anything with it was amazing. Seriously, the man was very clever. With that old microscope, Darwin observed many small details of a cell. But for him, the cell still looked simple enough to be explained by a theory of random mutations. Today we can see so much more, including the intricate detail, the DNA, the complex order, and information carried within each cell. So today, we really have no excuse at all."

"Sorry," Ethan said. "Darwin doesn't get a pass."

"You are so right, Ethan," Gen said. "In 900 BC, King David acknowledged how intricately and wonderfully he was made. That was centuries ago, yet he completely understood the extreme complexity of his inward parts."

"I'm guessing King David didn't have any kind of microscope at all," Ethan added. "Sorry, Joseph, I'd say Darwin is sunk!"

"So are most other scientists," Gen said. "They still believe we simply happened by chance, as though we are just the result of some freak cosmic accident."

"Speak for yourself," Raymond snickered.

Abi joined the conversation. "No matter how big of an impact this fossil will create, people will decide for themselves what to believe. Sometimes, a lie is easier."

Abruptly, David began to slow the car. "Whoa. Something's going on up ahead."

Brake lights flashed in front of them. The line of cars gradually came to a complete stop.

"It's a roadblock, Dad," Ethan said. "Looks like two squad cars are stopping everyone."

David cautiously pulled up in line with the other cars. Approximately fourteen cars were in front of them. Four uniformed officers manned the roadblock. They were talking to each driver and inspecting each vehicle before letting them drive ahead.

"Now they have the police working for them?" Ethan groaned.

"They receive a call from their superiors," Abi said, "and simply follow orders. This must be some of the 'additional resources' Dr. Emery was talking about. The man with the crew cut evidently couldn't make it here soon enough."

David hit redial on his phone and waited a moment for the secretary to connect him. "Mr. Sterner, is that bird in the air yet? No, I have no idea how many breaking stories you have today . . . Yes, I'm sure it is difficult to find another pilot on a moment's notice. Here's the situation. The competition is fairly close. They are very big and have a lot of disposable income . . . Yes, I believe they are listening to these phone calls . . . No, it's not CNN."

David ended the call. "No chance that the news crew will be here in the next five minutes." He watched as the officers searched the car in the front of the line.

"Apparently, these patrolmen don't know what the type of car we're driving." He looked in his rearview mirror. "Joseph, hand Ethan a black marker from my glove box. Ethan, grab one of these maps. I want you to write in letters big enough to be read by the car behind us."

Confused, Ethan unfolded a large section of a map.

"Write, 'Would you like to make?' . . . wait." David opened his wallet. "I've got one hundred and fifty. What else do we have?"

Everyone dug into their pockets. "Twenty here." "I've got ten . . ."

"Write, in very big letters," David said, "'Would you like to make two hundred dollars?' Now hold that up in the back window so the driver can read it."

The man in the car behind them leaned forward slightly to read the sign. He edged his car a bit closer. Ethan took down the sign and looked at him. He was young, perhaps a college student. Perfect. Most college students are broke. He looked slightly bemused and shrugged his shoulders. Then he nodded yes.

"He said yes!" Ethan shouted, still unsure what was happening.

By this time, they were just eight cars from the roadblock and checkpoint.

"Now write this," Ethan's dad said hurriedly. "'U-turn, and drive back two miles!'"

"That's it?" Ethan said.

"Yes. Write that. Hurry!"

Ethan wrote the sentence in big letters on another map. He held it up to the rear window.

The young man behind them looked very confused. He scrunched up his face while pondering this odd request. One more car passed through the roadblock. The young man looked up at Ethan, thought a while longer, and then held up two fingers. Then he rubbed his fingers against his thumb.

"I think he's agreed to do it," Ethan said. "He's displaying the universal sign for 'show me the money.'"

Ethan collected the two hundred dollars from the group and reached for the door handle.

"Wait!" Ethan's dad yelled. "We're too close to the checkpoint to use the door. Ethan, Gen, scrunch to the side and fold down one seat. Raymond, you're my man. You should be small enough to crawl back to the trunk. Don't worry, I'll release it from here. Ethan, give him the money."

"Sweet," Raymond said.

One more car cleared the checkpoint.

"Just don't let the trunk lid swing all the way open. When I pop it open, catch it from the inside."

Ethan and Gen squeezed halfway against the front seats and all the way to one side. As always, Gen held the green bag tightly on her lap. She was careful not to damage the precious contents. Raymond managed to fold down one of the seats. Within seconds he crawled through the small opening and into the trunk. Another car passed the checkpoint. David hit the trunk release and Raymond grabbed the bottom of the lid as instructed. He opened it just wide enough to crawl out before gently closing it. Staying low, he took only three steps to the car behind him. He was stuck, unsure about his next move. He didn't want to sneak around to the driver's side door. The police officers would see him for sure. He looked back at Ethan. Ethan signaled for him to freeze.

"Joseph, tell me when the officers are looking away," Ethan said.

"Not now," Joseph said. "One more car just went through. No . . . no . . . no . . . Now! *Go!*"

Ethan waved frantically at Raymond. Dropping to the road, Raymond preformed some crazy sort of barrel roll, ending up next to the door. The young driver looked highly amused, rolled down his window, and then happily reached down to grab the cash. Raymond quickly returned to the trunk, staying low and out of sight. David pressed the trunk release—but nothing happened.

"Open the trunk, Dad," Ethan pleaded.

"It won't release. Raymond didn't latch it tight enough."

Only three cars remained between them and the officers. David left a gap between his car and the car in front of them. He was afraid to pull any farther forward, even though that in itself might raise a red flag.

Ethan turned toward Raymond. He placed both his hands on the backseat and mimicked pressing down hard on the lid. Raymond looked perplexed at first. Finally, he figured it out and pushed on the trunk gently in an effort to be quiet. No luck. The second time, he jumped slightly off the road, using most of his weight on the way down. As soon as David heard the latch catch, he hit the release button. Raymond caught the lid and crawled back into the trunk and through to the backseat.

"Awesome," Ethan said. Gen gave her little brother a big hug.

Raymond was flushed. "At least now I know what I want to be when I grow up: a Ninja."

The group laughed, but only briefly. Their unusual activity caught the attention of one of the officers, who was now walking steadily toward their car. About the same moment, the young man in the car behind them decided the time was right to earn his money. He backed up slightly before giving Ethan a wave, and then pulled off a very fast and impressive U-turn. He hit the gas and sped off in the opposite direction. The officer who was nearly to David's car turned and ran back to his squad car. The other officers also jumped into their cars and set their sirens to blaring. Off they went, chasing the young man who was two hundred dollars richer. The cars that were waiting in line paused for a few moments, and then all began to drive ahead, David's car included. They cleared the checkpoint and drove on.

"I'm really starting to enjoy this," Joseph said.

"I'm not," Abi said. "We must be crazy risking the safety of a little boy like that, not to mention a stranger! What's going to happen to him when they catch up? Where is that news helicopter anyway?"

Ethan searched the sky for any sign of a helicopter and news team. This news team and its chopper was critical to the plan. With every passing second, the chances increased that the fossil would never make an appearance on the evening news.

"The officers that took after our friend with the two hundred dollars won't be gone long," David said. "I'm guessing that they pulled him over and were a bit disappointed to discover that he was all alone. Don't worry, Abi; the kid probably won't even get a ticket, maybe just a quick scolding. The officers will be back in a hurry, and they might even know what kind of car we're driving now."

"We were lucky that time," Abi said. "Maybe we should get off the road while we wait for the helicopter."

David agreed, and quickly found a narrow crossroad surrounded by a huge grove of tall pine trees. He turned onto the small road and parked the Buick as far under the trees as he could. "Everyone out. Find a spot where you're not visible from the main road, but where we can keep a lookout for the news chopper. Once we spot it, we all need to wave and jump around like crazy. Hopefully they will see us."

With so many tall pines, finding a spot to watch the entire sky was impossible. Even though Seattle was southwest of their location, no one knew exactly where the helicopter would first appear. Ethan chose a spot where he could see well to the south and west. Gen was not too far away, looking to the northwest. All that was left for them to do was to wait.

Ethan could see the main road from his location. Sirens still blaring, the two squad cars had returned. They zipped by, heading back toward Seattle. Good thing David had made the decision to get off the road.

"Look!" Joseph shouted. He was pointing southwest, into the sky. Ethan shielded his eyes from the sun. Sure enough, a black dot in the sky was heading their way. Too small to identify yet, but it was not an airplane.

"That's it!" Raymond yelled. "Yes!" He and his sister ran out of the trees heading for the main road. They were joined by Abi and Joseph, who were already furiously waving their arms.

Ethan peered closely at the approaching aircraft. It was a helicopter. That was great news. However, he also noticed another dot in the sky. Slightly behind, a second helicopter was traveling in the same direction. Something wasn't right. He looked anxiously for Gen and Raymond. They were with the rest of their group, already on the shoulder of the main road.

Ethan looked again into the sky. The first helicopter was getting close enough that he should be able to see some sort of markings or a TV logo. None were visible. He had a bad feeling.

"Stop," he shouted. "Get off the road!"

Everyone stopped and looked back at Ethan.

"That's not the TV chopper!" Ethan yelled. "Get back here now!"

Without hesitation, they all ran back to the trees as quickly as they could.

"Who is it? Are you sure it's not the TV crew?" David said.

"I don't know," Ethan said as the helicopters flew closer. "Look, they're all black, with no identification at all. Emery was right when he said they were serious about retrieving the fossil."

The helicopters slowed, pausing not more than one hundred yards away. They looked like two black dragonflies hovering over a field, hoping to scare up some bugs to devour. At times the aircraft pointed their noses toward the ground. At other times the black choppers turned toward the other.

"I should call Mr. Sterner," David said.

"Not now," Ethan said. "The news crew has to have a general idea where we are. If you make a call now with those choppers so close, they can zero in on us for sure."

"But they might be from the station," Abi said. "This is exactly what we have been waiting for."

The choppers edged closer to their location. Everyone pressed as tightly as they could against several trees. The blades' loud *thup-thup-thup-thup* was unnerving. The treetops around them danced wildly.

"No way they're TV choppers," Raymond said. "TV choppers are always covered with the station's logo, or big bright call letters, or even the anchor's face. The TV stations get free advertising wherever those things go."

"You're right," Abi said. "No one move."

The group remained frozen under the protection of the tall pine trees. Eventually, the choppers slowly moved away, heading up the road. Ethan stepped cautiously away from the trees in order to track them. He was covered in pine needles, as were the others.

"The helicopters are landing," Ethan said. "They landed right on the road, only about two miles ahead."

"Another roadblock," Joseph said. "Now what do we do?"

"We still have the fossil," David said. "We are still playing keep-away. I say we head nonchalantly back in the other direction. And like you said, Gen, pray that the TV crew finds us first."

CHAPTER FIFTEEN

I believe that unarmed truth and unconditional love will have the final word in reality. This is why right, temporarily defeated, is stronger than evil triumphant.

—Martin Luther King Jr.[12]

David eased the Buick back onto the road, heading away from the squad cars and the black helicopters. He checked his rearview mirror frequently. Since five other people were doing the exact same thing, he wouldn't have had to bother. He really wasn't going anywhere. He was simply keeping as much distance as he could between the fossil and the black helicopters for as long as possible. The fossil had to be kept in play until the news crew arrived.

"Everyone doing all right?" David asked.

"Great, just great," Ethan answered. "At least we haven't seen the guy with the crew cut. We'd really have something to worry about then."

"I will be feeling a whole lot better when we see the Sterner Broadcasting helicopter," Abi said.

"That is true," Joseph said. "But man, am I impressed."

"What on earth are you talking about?" David asked.

"The State Department, or Homeland Security, or whoever is chasing us, might not even know what we are driving, yet they seem to be closing in fast."

"And that is a good thing? How is that good thing?" Ethan asked.

"Not for us maybe," Joseph said, "but I feel much better about our country's ability to track terrorists. They are doing a fine job."

Everyone looked at Joseph like he was from a different planet.

"OK, props for tracking," Ethan said, "but a major fail on identifying real terrorists."

"Just giving credit where credit is due," said Joseph. "I'm just really nervous waiting for the news helicopter. I am trying to think of something positive."

"Joseph's right," David said. "This is making us all nuts. We need to know the location of that news crew." David picked up his phone.

Ethan wasn't sure if this was wise. One more call might reveal their exact location. At the same time, to get a fix on the news helicopter would be extremely useful.

"Mr. Sterner, the story is still up for grabs but the window is closing fast . . . That is good to hear. We've had a slight change of plans and are now headed the other direction on Highway 92 . . . Good enough, but please tell them to step on it." David ended the call.

"What's up with Sterner Broadcasting?" Ethan asked.

"The bird is in the air," David said. "Mr. Sterner says the news team is headed our way and will be here soon. He also said this story better be worth it."

From this point on, there was no more hiding. Everything was on the line. Sterner Broadcasting had to get to them first—end of story. It was that simple. No one wanted to think about the alternative. Their adventure was nearing its end. But, by far, the most dangerous stretch remained.

Gen reached for Ethan's hand. He noticed she was also holding Raymond's hand. Her eyes were closed, and she quietly moved her lips. She was praying. If Gen thought prayer was important, perhaps he should try it too. He wasn't sure what to say. Should he pray for safety, for the news helicopter to find them first, maybe for the man with the crew cut to get hit by a truck?

He closed his eyes and prayed what he felt. *Dear God, these last few days have been amazing. Thank you for them. Thank you for bringing back my mom and my dad. Thank you for all that has happened, in order for me to be a better person, to help me grow. I used to think it was all about me, even though most of the time I felt worthless and empty. Now I can see it's not about me, it's really about You. Yet, I feel much more important—like I really do matter. Thank you, God, and help me be more like Gen.*

Ethan opened his eyes and looked at the road ahead. There was only one other car on the road, traveling in the same direction. The two-lane road rolled gently over small hills. Alternating patches of pine trees and fields bordered the road. No homes appeared alongside the road. No cars came into view from the other direction. Seemed a bit odd. Clearly, a lot less traffic was traveling this highway than earlier, but perhaps that was normal.

Ethan looked out the back window and scanned the sky. Nothing but a smooth sheet of gray clouds. Without the sun, Ethan had completely lost track of the time. *Too quiet*, he thought. This was the calm before the storm, and Ethan was convinced a storm was coming. Perhaps the black helicopters would arrive first and force them off the road. Maybe the man with the crew cut and the weird whisper voice would make an appearance. All because of a fossil, one medium-sized dinosaur bone holding a sliver of truth. How odd that the truth could be so dangerous, so threatening.

Ethan leaned back into his seat. He had no idea what would happen next. But for some reason, this did not bother him. This was strange; something inside was different. He did not feel afraid or anxious. He was in precisely the right place at the right time. Ethan did not know how to describe it, like he was part of something important. He looked at Gen and smiled. He was beginning to understand. No matter what happened, God was in charge, and he felt completely at peace.

"There they are!" Raymond shouted. "Two helicopters directly behind us."

Sure enough, two small black dots in the sky were quickly growing larger. Within seconds they were clearly identifiable as helicopters.

David sat up straighter and regripped the steering wheel. "Raymond, do you see anything else?"

Raymond's quick eyes searched the sky behind the car. "Nothing."

"No reason at this point to try and hide," David said. "Our only hope is that our news helicopter will show up and disrupt their plans." He accelerated. "We might as well prolong our encounter with the two helicopters as long as possible. Even a few seconds could make all the difference."

The silver Buick was really moving now. The speedometer pushed toward eighty-five. The two black helicopters did not seem to be impressed and were gaining quickly. No one spoke. Everyone held their breath. No sign of any other helicopter surfaced. The car began to shudder as the speedometer moved toward ninety.

The Buick was approaching the steamroller and bulldozer on the side of the road, right where they had left them. Ethan saw something else as well. His dad must have spotted it at the same time. Two black SUVs suddenly pulled onto the road, blocking both lanes of the highway. David hit the brakes hard and struggled to keep the car under control. The tires screeched wildly, while smoke billowed behind the car. Everyone was slammed forward and caught hard by their seat belts while hanging onto anything they could. Like it or not, the car came to a stop thirty feet in front of the ominous black SUVs.

"Everyone still with us?" David asked quickly. He didn't wait for a response but looked in his rearview mirror for an exit. There was none. The two black helicopters landed directly on the road, twenty feet behind them.

The journey had come to an end.

Everything was still. No one moved. The dark tinted windows of the black SUVs seemed to be staring at them, as though cold and emotionless.

Raymond looked out the back window one more time, hoping to see the TV helicopter. "In case anyone's wondering, there's no sign of the cavalry yet," he said quietly.

All eight doors of the black SUVs opened at once. The man with the blond crew cut, along with seven others, stepped out. They were all dressed in beige or dark blue pants and loose jackets. Ethan was sure they were armed. They all had on the standard-issue sunglasses, which hardly seemed appropriate for a day in which there was little sun. Seven of the men spread out along the sides of the road. The man with the crew cut walked up and stood in front of David's car. He took off his sunglasses and cleared his throat.

"Everyone out. Now!" he said in his loud, icy whisper.

They all hesitated for a moment, wondering if they had any option but to comply with the order.

"Here we go," David said. "Cooperation might be our best option at this point." He opened his door and climbed out. The others followed suit, but slowly. As they lined up next to the car, Ethan couldn't help notice a large bump on Whisper Man's forehead. Most likely from his close encounter with a T. rex.

The man cleared his throat once again before speaking. "Might I ask what you have done with Professor Emery?"

"He took a slight detour. I believe he's run into a bit of engine trouble," David said.

"No matter. Dr. Emery is not my primary concern. I must say your efforts have been most impressive, all of you.

Mr. Booker, Dr. Booker, Joseph, young girl, young boy who has a good deal of nerve, and especially you, master Ethan. You are an odd group to say the least. We have been at this now for more than three weeks. Yes, you were predictable. Everyone is. You, however, were able to avoid the inevitable for at least a few days. As I said, I am impressed. I am also very confused. I will never understand, for example, why you tried so hard to protect a bone. That is beyond me."

He slowly turned his head from side to side, most likely loosening his sore neck. "And speaking of the bone, I need to see it now."

Gen still carried the green baseball equipment bag over her shoulder. She stepped toward the man and unzipped the bag. Watching her reach in the bag and pull out the wrapped bone was more than painful. Ethan winced as she handed it to him.

Ethan glanced skyward. No sign of the Sterner Broadcasting news chopper.

The man cleared his throat and walked back toward the SUVs. He stopped and unwrapped the bundle on the hood of one of the SUVs. He held the bone in his hands. Ethan could not imagine how hard this must be for his mother.

The man looked toward Ethan. "Young man, I know you would most enjoy being some sort of hero. I will give you that opportunity." He looked at the heavy equipment on the side of the road. "Since the bulldozer uncovered this and started all this fuss, I believe that a steamroller should end it. Heavy machinery from start to end. I find that rather fitting." He placed the bone in the middle of the road.

"Go ahead, Ethan. Climb up on that steamroller and start it up. The honor is all yours."

Ethan felt so helpless, so defeated. He looked back at his family, partly for support and partly as a way of saying he was terribly sorry for what he was about to do. His feet carried him up the steps of the steamroller, but his mind was elsewhere. *How can this be happening if God is in control? Is all this some sort of*

a game for God's amusement? Does He enjoy watching us run
for our lives for no reason? Why did we fight so hard for days to
protect this fossil that holds the truth if only to watch the bone get
destroyed in the middle of a road?

The man with the crew cut shifted his feet impatiently. He
reached into his jacket and produced a pistol. "Quit stalling,
young man. Start the machine."

Ethan was not stalling on purpose. He had never been
in the cab of the steamroller before. Having a pistol waved
in the air did not help his ability to focus on the controls.
David understood the situation and took a step toward the
machine, only to be stopped by an icy "Not another step!"

The controls were not that different from the bulldozer.
Ethan discovered the ignition key down below the steering
wheel and started the engine, much to the relief of his father.
The huge machine roared to life, but Ethan did not hear the
noise. He could not bear to look into the faces of Gen or his
mother as he shifted the steamroller into the forward gear and
steered it onto the road. The blacktop noisily cracked as the
massive roller compressed and fractured the surface. Ethan
strained hard to turn the wheel and aim directly at the bone
lying harmlessly on the blacktop ahead.

And then he thought: *This can't be right. This is a mistake.*
The TV crew will come. I have to stall as long as possible.
Ethan shifted the machine out of gear and turned it off.
An eerie silence engulfed the group. The other seven men
around Whisper Man took a menacing step forward as
though ready to react.

Gen turned around to look into the sky. Perhaps Ethan
had spotted the TV helicopter. Nothing there. When she
turned back, the man with the crew cut was on her. In an
instant he grabbed Gen around the waist and placed his re-
volver against her head. Abi screamed.

The man with the crew cut looked calmly at Ethan. He
pressed the barrel hard against Gen's temple, making her
wince. "Now!" he shouted in his icy voice.

Ethan did not hesitate. Nothing else mattered anymore, nothing but Gen. His hands shook as he turned the key. The huge machine's engine turned over—but would not start.

"Ethan," shouted the man with the crew cut, "I will begin with this one! Next, your mom!"

"It's . . . it's flooded," stammered David. "He is not familiar with this machine. Please, let me climb up there. I'll crush that bone."

Whisper Man told Ethan's dad to step away.

Ethan tried again. The engine roared to life. Thick black smoke poured out of the smokestack. Ethan shifted as quickly as he could. The machine lurched forward as the roller devoured the bone quickly and efficiently. He could not hear the crushing of the bone over the noise of the machine, but he could feel the spirits of the group crumble. He could not look at them.

"Back again!" Whisper Man yelled so he could be heard over the steamroller's engine.

Ethan shifted into reverse and rolled back. When he was once again off the road, he looked for the bone. Nothing was left but a broken road surface with a gray streak of sand and dust that was quickly blowing away in the wind.

Two of the men wearing sunglasses moved toward the dusty spot on the road, studied the debris, and nodded their approval. The man with the crew cut released his grip on Gen and pushed her back toward the others by the car. "That wasn't so hard, was it?"

Ethan climbed down from the cab. "It's done. So now what?"

"Now? Should there be something more? As I told you all along, we simply needed the bone. Or should I say, we needed to destroy it. Nothing more is left to do. You were in the way. You put yourselves and your friends in a lot of danger for nothing."

"You're saying we can just go?" Abi said.

"The bone is destroyed. That was our objective. To be honest, I don't care what you do next. Perhaps you want to tell your story to the world. From what I've been told, no one is worried about that. Apparently, if you start speaking about some nonexistent fossil with a spearhead, you will immediately be labeled . . . let me think . . . I believe the expression is a 'nut job.' You will become irrelevant. You see, the people I work for are very smart. They are in control. And when you are able to control the way people think, you can be very powerful indeed."

Suddenly, they heard the unmistakable sound of an approaching helicopter. As it grew closer, the words Sterner Broadcasting, painted in huge orange letters, were clearly visible.

The two black helicopters immediately fired up their engines. They quickly rose into the air and twisted their noses away. The men loaded into their black SUVs. They had nothing to say. Just as quickly, they turned around and drove off. Like a receding black tide, all of them disappeared.

CHAPTER SIXTEEN

God creates out of nothing. Wonderful you say.
Yes, to be sure, but he does what is still more
wonderful: he makes saints out of sinners.
—Soren Kierkegaard[13]

The Sterner Broadcasting helicopter found a place to land in an open field just off the road. Ethan just shook his head. *Ten minutes. Seriously, how hard would it have been to arrive ten minutes earlier? No doubt someone needed that one more cup of coffee or maybe had to finish that doughnut.* "What a waste!" Ethan groaned out loud as he stared at the dusty spot on the cracked road surface. Everything did seem like a complete waste. Everything seemed meaningless.

Ethan realized that Gen needed a hug. Unfortunately, he would have to wait his turn as Raymond had his arms wrapped completely around his brave sister. No problem; Ethan decided a group hug was perfect. He noticed that his mom and dad were also hugging each other. That was interesting. Someone needed to hug Joseph pretty soon.

Ethan let go of Gen and Raymond and joined his mom and dad. "I'm so sorry, Mom. We lost your fossil. I can't believe it. We fought so hard to keep it. We lost. Your fossil is gone, and I'm the one who destroyed it."

Long streaks were visible on Abi's cheeks. She had been crying. In spite of what happened only moments ago, she smiled at her handsome son. "Don't worry about it, Ethan," she said as she held his face in her hands. "The important thing is—"

Ethan finished her sentence: "—that we're alive. Yes, Mom, I know."

Two people from the helicopter made their way to the middle of the road not far from the last remaining signs of the bone. A third person, likely the pilot, remained in the cockpit. One of the men, wearing blue jeans, had a camera strapped to his shoulder. The second guy wore a dark sport coat and a bright orange tie. He was very concerned about his hair, which apparently had been mussed by the chopper. A microphone stuck out of one of his coat pockets. Obviously, he was the reporter. He looked confused and unsure as he approached the dusty, tired-looking collection of adults and children.

"Apparently, we landed in the wrong place," the reporter said. "We are looking for a scientific team lead by a Mr. David Booker."

"I'm Mr. Booker," David said.

"Interesting. I received the most curious phone call from Mr. J. Sterner. He said I needed to drop everything, fly down Highway 92, and somehow find Mr. David Booker. Mr. Sterner was very clear with me that you would have a big story. Just for the record, Mr. David Booker, I have been a reporter for twenty years. Let's just say, I'm skeptical. You and your entourage do not exude 'big story' to me. But go ahead, surprise me."

"What I told Mr. Sterner," David said, trying hard to control his anger, "was if you got here in time, you would get your story. You had to get here first. Second place gets nothing."

"You mean those other guys?" the reporter said. "You sold your story to the folks in the black cars and helicopters?

That slick group had government written all over it. I'm not sure what you are up to, Mr. David Booker, but I'm calling Mr. Sterner right now. This is outrageous. Do you have any idea how much money it costs to send a helicopter crew way out here on a moment's notice? I have a feeling you might be hearing from our lawyers."

The reporter with the great hair pulled a phone out of his pocket and dialed. "Yeah, Barbara, this is Ian. Get me the big guy." He waited impatiently, looking terribly annoyed. "Mr. Sterner, this is Ian. No, no, nothing. We have a big prob—" He wasn't able to finish the sentence as David snatched the phone out of his hand.

"Mr. Sterner, this is David. No, there will be no story." Ian attempted to reclaim his phone. Dad simply held him away with one arm. "Your boys were about ten minutes too late . . . I'm sorry, too, but I told you very plainly that I couldn't promise anything. Believe me, it was a chance worth taking. Maybe someday I'll tell you about it sitting around your pond . . . Thank you, sir. I'll hand the phone back to Ian now."

"Here's your story." Dad turned to the dusty spot on the cracked road and pointed.

For an instant, the cameraman was interested. He immediately started filming. Once he saw what David pointed to, he shut off the camera. Ian's face was nearly purple. David shrugged his shoulders and walked away.

Before the reporter turned to leave, Gen suddenly stepped forward. "Actually, you are not too late. Mr. Booker, could you open your trunk for me?"

Ethan's head started to spin. Everyone looked confused—except Abi. She was smiling.

"Does anyone really know what's going on around here?" Ian asked. "Do we have a story or not?"

Gen reached into the trunk, pulled back the door on a compartment between the main truck and backseat, and produced a three-foot-long bundle wrapped in a towel from the hotel. She carefully opened the towel and held in her hands the fossilized femur of an allosaurus—complete with a spearhead.

What a shame the cameraman was not filming. Raymond, Ethan, Joseph, and David all had the same expression. Mouths agape, eyes bugged out of their heads. All of them were trying to speak, but only parts of words came out. "Wha . . .?" "Bu . . ." were the most common.

"Nice switch," Abi said quietly, calmly, with a slight smile.

"I can't believe you stole a towel from the hotel!" Raymond cried.

Within seconds, the cameraman started filming. Ian smoothed his hair one last time and took the microphone out of his pocket. "Fine," he said. "We will edit all of this later, but let's see what we can do."

He cleared his throat and took three long, slow breaths. The camera was rolling. "This is Ian Walters for the Sterner Broadcasting Network with an exclusive report. We are standing here on Highway 92, about seventy miles from Seattle. Standing next to me is Mr. David Booker. Mr. Booker, will you explain this item to our viewers. Some sort of a fossil? Do I have that correct?"

"Ian, wait. Just wait. Turn off that camera." David walked over to face Geneva Hartmann. "How, Gen? How is this possible?"

"Science," she said. "Actually, Dr. Emery gave me the idea. Remember how he said that it was difficult to tell the difference between replica fossils and the real fossils? He was right."

"You mean to say," Joseph said, "the fossil that Ethan crushed with that noisy machine was a fake?"

"That sums it up," Gen said. "Completely fake."

"But, but . . ." stuttered Ethan. "Where, when, uh . . . how did you get it?"

"I took it from the bone room in the museum. While everyone was busy running around, I simply grabbed a femur. Dr. Emery had helped by pointing one out, remember?"

"But . . . why?" Ethan asked. "What made you even think about grabbing a bone?"

"I just had a feeling," she said, smiling at Ethan. "You just never know when a fake dinosaur femur might come in handy."

Ethan just shook his head. "You are so far out of my league, it's ridiculous."

"Why didn't you tell us before?" Abi asked.

"I certainly thought about it," said Gen, handing the fossil carefully to Abi. "But I knew if I really tried to switch fossils, a fair amount of plausible deniability wouldn't hurt."

Ethan scrunched up his face. "Plausi-what?"

Gen smiled. "The look on your faces when Ethan flattened the bone was perfect. Whisper Guy was completely fooled. Sorry to do that to you, but your expressions could not be faked. Except for you, Dr. Booker. You did a fine acting job. I knew you would realize that the steamroller was not crushing the real fossil. Good thing everyone else was fooled. Undoubtedly it convinced Whisper Guy and his friends."

"Unbelievable," Ethan said.

"Gen, you had a gun to your head," Joseph said.

"I'd be lying if I said I wasn't scared. And maybe I got way more scared when Ethan flooded the engine. But I figured God brought us this far. I trusted that He would see us safely through to the end."

"All right, enough of this," Ian said. "I have no idea what you people are talking about. All I know is I need a story. A big story. Can I please interview someone now?"

"Certainly," David said. "I'll let my . . . my wife do the honors. Dr. Abigail Booker."

Ian sighed, but then started the take over again. "Dr. Abigail Booker, you are in possession of some sort of rare fossil. Can you describe it for our viewers?"

"I would love to," Abi said, beaming at Gen. "This is a fossilized femur of an allosaurus. An allosaurus was a large and very fierce meat-eating dinosaur."

"Clearly, this must be a very rare find," Ian said, clearly trying to quickly hype the story.

"Not really," Abi said. "I believe over fifty allosaurus skeletons have been excavated and reconstructed. Most of them are in museums throughout the world."

Ian once again was getting annoyed. "I had the impression that this fossil was unusual. Is this an unusual find, Dr. Booker?"

Abi smiled. The rest of the group smiled with her. "It is most unusual. This fossil will change everything. You see, on this side of the femur"—she turned the fossil over—"a prehistoric spearhead is lodged deep into the bone."

"She is correct," Joseph shouted from off camera. "I am Joseph Nori, and I concur with Dr. Booker."

Ian motioned for the cameraman to swing around to get Joseph in the shot.

"I myself have had the privilege of examining this fossil. Indeed, a spearhead, made of obsidian, is lodged into the fossil. Evidence of new bone growth surrounding the head of the spear indicates the allosaurus was alive when the spear struck it."

"Dr. Booker?" Ian interrupted "Are you a paleontologist?"

"I am," Abi said, "although I haven't done field work for some time."

"I have," Joseph said. "I am also a real paleontologist."

Ian once again was looking highly annoyed. "Turn off the camera," he said. "Look, I am not a paleontologist. However, I did take Biology 101 in college, and even I know that dinosaurs and humans did not live at the same time. Not even close! This is a farce. Why don't you make your own video and post it on YouTube? Who do you people think you are?"

"This is for real," David said. "That's why this is such a big story. Don't you see, we need to get this story out there on TV. People need to know about this."

"I don't know," Ian said. "Seems like I'm wasting my time. No offense, Dr. Booker, but I've never heard of you. Our station is very careful about reporting pranks. You know, crop circles that were really made by two kids with a two-by-four—that sort of thing. One time we responded to a report of aliens attacking downtown Seattle. Turns out, the *Star Trek* convention was in town."

"Oh, yes," Joseph said. "That was a good one."

"What will it take for you to take us seriously?" David asked.

"Some authority. You know, someone that is respected."

As if on cue, Dr. Emery stumbled out of the trees. He looked confused and disheveled. He still wore a tie, but it hung over his shoulder and down his back. His shirt had lost a button and one sleeve was torn. His glasses were on his face, but they were bent and crooked.

"We're in luck," Ethan said. "Here comes Dr. Emery. He's the head of paleontology at the Museum of Natural History in Seattle." Ethan grimaced as he played his bluff. "He's part of our, uh . . . team." Ethan motioned to his father for help.

The cameraman swung around to film Dr. Emery wandering toward the group.

"I am familiar with Dr. Emery," Ian said. "I've interviewed him several times. He's like the top authority as far as dinosaurs are concerned. Uh, by the way . . . what's the matter with him?"

David ran to the professor's side and put his arm around him. Ethan could tell that David gripped the doctor tighter than was necessary, as a bit of a reminder. David led Dr. Emery to Ian. The reporter straightened the professor's tie and tried to neaten up his shirt. "Yes, we are happy to have Dr. Emery on our team," David said. "His expertise is only matched by his dedication. Why, he has been here doing fieldwork for the last few days. Right, Doctor?"

The vise-like grip around his shoulders served as an effective prompt.

"Uh, yes. Fieldwork. Assisting Dr. Booker here with fieldwork."

Ian motioned to the fossil in Abi's hands. "Dr. Emery, have you examined this bone?"

Dr. Emery looked at the fossil. He looked at Abi and once again felt the grip around his shoulders. "Yes, I have had the opportunity to examine it."

"What can you tell us about it?" Ian asked.

"It is most likely a femur from an allosaurus."

Abi turned the fossil over, revealing the spearhead. "If you would, Dr. Emery, what can you tell us about this item lodged into the dinosaur bone?"

David released his grip, allowing Dr. Emery to stand on his own. That was good. There was no way that this moment would be sullied by any hint of intimidation. The next statement out of Dr. Emery's mouth had the potential to alter the course of science and to shake up many lives that had turned away from the truth. Plus, it was possible that Dr. Emery still retained a shred of integrity.

"Dr. Emery?" the reporter repeated.

This was the moment of truth. The professor hesitated. The once distinguished man appeared beaten, not simply because of a rough day in his Range Rover, but beaten down by years of conformity, years of denying the evidence he felt in his soul. Now he was tired, hungry, and broken. He no longer had the energy or strength to defend a lie. He looked down at the fossil, and then over at Abi. Suddenly he held his head a bit higher, his eyes brightening.

"That item lodged in the fossil is a spearhead. Without a doubt, this allosaurus was alive when a human being tried to kill it with a spear. I understand this does not coexist with our current, acceptable view on evolution. What can I say? I am a scientist." He adjusted his glasses. "We must always remember: the fundamental and ultimate goal of science is to reveal the truth, not control it."

Ian stopped the interview and immediately dialed a number on his phone. "Sara, get ready for some fast editing. We'll be uploading video from the chopper in the next two minutes. Tell Mr. Sterner that we do indeed have a story . . . Yes, just barge in and tell him. This is breaking news. You need to have this ready to run in sixty minutes. Yes, start running a banner now: 'Exclusive footage, Shocking scientific discovery.' Something along those lines. Got that? OK, we're leaving right now."

The Sterner Broadcasting news crew turned to start back to the helicopter. Ian stopped to shout: "Dr. Booker, call us later to arrange an interview at the studio. You too, Dr. Emery."

"I will be there also!" Joseph called.

Ian paused and then walked closer to Abi. "This could actually change things, couldn't it?" he asked her.

"Oh, yes," she said. "For the better."

"Take care of that bone," he said. "Look, here's my business card. Contact me in the next twenty-four hours. We'll want to do follow-up interviews."

"I think it is safe now," Abi said. She knew that once news of the fossil was broadcast to the world, there would be no point in destroying it. With that, Ian smiled at her, and then jogged to the chopper. In a matter of seconds, the bird was in the air.

They all just stood there, watching until the helicopter disappeared.

"Can we go home now?" Raymond asked.

"An excellent idea," David said as they all headed for the Buick.

Ethan stopped. "Uh, what about the professor?"

Dr. Emery stood by the side of the road, still looking a bit dazed.

"It's OK with me if he comes with us," David said. "We did sort of mess up his car. Abi, you should be the one to make the decision."

Abi approached the professor. "Thank you," was all she could say, at first.

His eyes glistened as he looked at her. "No, Dr. Booker, thank you. Today you set me free. However, you did wreck my car. So, yes, I would love a ride home."

"All right!" David said. "Let's go. Of course, we will be one seat short."

"No problem," Gen said. "Raymond is pretty good at getting into the trunk."

"Worst babysitter ever," Raymond mumbled.

∞ ∞ ∞ ∞ ∞ ∞ ∞

Four days later . . .
The man with the blond crew cut and an icy voice was sitting in a massive leather chair in front of a large television. He was in the middle of a heated conversation with someone on his phone.

"Of course I have seen the reports on the news. They are lying. I saw the fossil destroyed with my own eyes . . . What? . . . You sampled dust from the road? . . . Plastic resin?! There must be some mistake . . ."

Frost listened intently for a few minutes. His head and shoulders sagged as if he were slowly deflating. He cleared his throat. "I understand. Yes, even though the discovery of the fossil has been made public, eliminating it is worth any cost. Once the bone is gone, people will once again have no proof, and soon will forget . . . No, too difficult right now."

He continued: "Plans are to allow the public to view the fossil. When that happens, all we need to do is place one of our people as a security guard. No, I won't require a lot of resources, but I will not be able to do this myself. I will be recognized. But be assured, I will take care of it."

He rubbed his eyes and looked up at his television to see yet another report on the amazing discovery. He spoke one last time into his phone.

"Yes sir. I was defeated by a group of kids and three untrained adults . . . No, it won't happen again."

CHAPTER SEVENTEEN

*Faith is not belief without proof, but trust
without reservation.*
                                        —D. Elton Trueblood[14]

*F*ive months later . . .
The entrance to the large building was bathed in light,
illuminating lizards and other creatures carved out of stone.
Dr. Abigail Booker walked confidently to the front of the
building, shielding her eyes for a moment. This would be a
live shot. She appeared poised and relaxed as she looked at
the camera, waiting for her cue.

In the five months since the Hobbs Point Fossil first hit
television screens all over the world, Abigail Booker had become a bit of a celebrity. Sterner Broadcasting recognized
the opportunity and hired Dr. Booker as its new science
correspondent. The decision paid off handsomely for
J. Sterner while also giving Abi a huge audience.

The cameraman signaled her. She was on.

"This is Dr. Abigail Booker, science correspondent for
the Sterner Broadcasting Corporation. As you can see, we
are here for the grand opening of the new exhibit at the Seattle Museum of Natural History. Let's move over here"—

she motioned gently for the cameraman to follow her as she walked—"to try to get a shot of the people waiting to get in. This is amazing. I hope you can see this; the line stretches for blocks. The people in the front of the line here camped out overnight."

Abi walked to a young man in line. "Good morning, I'm Dr. Abigail Booker."

"I'm Jeff, and may I say what an honor it is to meet you," the young man said.

Abi smiled. "Thank you. May I ask how long you have been waiting?"

"Since yesterday afternoon. Me and my friends here . . ." A large whoop from his entourage briefly interrupted the interview. "As I was saying, we brought sleeping bags, tunes, and lots of snacks."

"Looks like fun," Abi said. "Can you tell our viewers what you are waiting to see?"

"We're waiting to see the fossil. You know, the Hobbs Point Fossil, of course. The one you discovered, Dr. Booker. Can I get your autograph?"

Besides Abi's correspondent duties, she had been on TV twenty-six times in the last few months. First she was interviewed on the Sterner Broadcasting Network, then *Good Morning America*, and then the *Today* show. Abi even narrated an hour-long special on the Discovery Channel. She was a natural in front of the camera.

Later, numerous televised debates against renowned evolutionary scientists kept her busy. Some of the debates received a higher market share than *Monday Night Football*. The scientists debating against her consistently used the same arguments. One of the more common criticisms was that the fossil should be discarded due to mishandling. From the beginning, the fossil was ripped out of the ground by a bulldozer, never properly preserved, and, worst of all, handled by children. Some of the debaters even attacked Abi personally, accusing her of conspiring with Dr. Emery and

Mr. Sterner in order to concoct an elaborate tale, all to create a realistic but bogus fossil for the express purpose of making money. After all, the stock price of Sterner Broadcasting Corporation had tripled since it first reported the discovery. Advertising rates had gone through the roof. Plus, the Seattle Museum of Natural History would double its annual income the very first day the "phony" fossil was displayed to the public.

However, all of this was secondary to the simple fact that since dinosaurs lived millions and millions of years before man—everybody knew that—a fossil with a spearhead in it simply could not be. The Hobbs Point Fossil, simply put, was impossible. Abi always thought it ironic that scientists, who so fiercely promoted adaptation and changes in species, were themselves completely rigid and incapable of even changing their minds.

All of this had made her extremely busy, but Abi knew the publicity was invaluable.

"These people have to wait one more hour for the doors to open," Abi told her viewers. "They will get to see the Hobbs Point Fossil with their own eyes."

The crowd outside cheered loudly.

"However, Sterner Broadcasting has been granted a special favor by the Seattle Museum of Natural History. Dr. Emery, the creator of the new exhibit, has given us, the viewing audience, permission to see it first. In just thirty minutes, all of you watching will be the first ones to see this monumental exhibit. Plus, our cameras will have exclusive access to view the actual Hobbs Point Fossil. This is not to be missed. This is Doctor Abigail Booker, live from the Seattle Museum of Natural History." The camera's bright white light and red on-air light both went out.

∞ ∞ ∞ ∞ ∞ ∞ ∞

At the same time, Ethan and Dr. Emery were inside the museum making last-minute preparations. As Dr. Emery scurried around the new exhibit adjusting tiny details, Ethan provided any help necessary. Through the entire process, Ethan had worked closely with Dr. Emery to bring the display to life. It began with Ethan sharing with the professor and his mom every detail of the dream he'd had the night in the hotel. Dr. Emery thought it was perfect. Perhaps it wasn't an accident that when the exhibit neared completion, the primitive man leading the attack looked a lot like Ethan.

The scene depicted was just the way Ethan remembered. The giant lizard cut off by thick trees, with heavy broken branches lying on the ground. A group of humans shaking their spears, one human in front, knees bent as if preparing to spring. The dinosaur, approximately twice the height of the man, looking enraged at this annoying and puny threat. The massive head appeared even bigger with its mouth wide open, full of sharp teeth. The creature's leathery, smooth green skin rippled with muscle as its black, razor-like claws reached out to grab the hunter.

The battle was perfect, matching Ethan's dream—and perhaps matching reality. However, signs would be posted reminding people that this scene was not a representation of fact but an educated guess based on the evidence revealed by the discovery of the Hobbs Point Fossil. Dr. Emery told Ethan that he was not anxious to make the same mistake that others before him had made. Too often, museums would recreate prehistoric spectacles and portray them as fact. Visitors to the Seattle museum would be reminded to look at the evidence and decide for themselves.

Perhaps even more amazing than the new display was the new professor. Ethan was astounded as he watched the transformation of Dr. Emery. The man he first met was washed up, sold out, and basically dead to the world. Now, here was a man with a clear and unmistakable sense of purpose. He possessed a newfound drive and vitality that enabled him to work nearly nonstop as he painstakingly completed the elaborate exhibit. His passion was evident in the meticulous attention to detail in the display. And what a display it was: the full-size depiction of a group of humans attacking an allosaurus with their spears. This was an extraordinary scene. A short time ago it would have been unthinkable for a museum to portray a scenario like this.

Even with the fossil's discovery, the concept had still been ridiculed by the scientific community. Other museums had publicly scoffed at the exhibition. Dr. Emery himself had been expelled from the National Science Foundation, and he was recently removed from his position at the university. These changes didn't bother the professor in the least, which impressed Ethan all the more.

Ethan looked at the clock on the wall. "Forty-five minutes until opening, Dr. Emery."

What an exciting day. Ethan tried to comprehend the impact of this historic opening. Because of the discovery, many things had already changed. Some things, not so much. Most of the universities and museums had not budged from their evolutionary doctrine. Perhaps they were too big to change. More likely they were too entrenched, with their funding too deeply dependent on what had been a beneficial system. The high schools, middle schools, and elementary schools, however, had altered their science curricula radically. Any new information regarding the fossil was eagerly snatched up by the schools. Young people seemed to claim ownership of the discovery. In a sense, the fossil was theirs. They owned this new understanding of their origin.

Stores were unable to keep enough Hobbs Point Fossil lunch boxes on their shelves. The most popular video game of the year was Man vs. Dino: The Hobbs Point Battle. At least thirty local schools had signed up for field trips to the museum today. One look outside confirmed this fact, with yellow school buses parked as far as the eye could see. The future was now in the hands of the youth, and this generation was learning the truth. Ethan only hoped that the young fans would appreciate the fossil for its true meaning, and not just as a fad.

Gen walked over and grabbed Ethan by the arm. "Let's look at the fossil one more time before the opening." She and Ethan had been given unlimited access to the museum in preparation for the grand opening. They spent most of their weekends here with Ethan's mom.

They approached the display of the Hobbs Point Fossil. Protected in a locked acrylic case, the fossilized bone even had its own armed security guard. The guard looked fittingly intimidating with his cold stare, dark hair, mustache, and broad shoulders.

"How's it going?" Ethan asked.

"Fine," the guard responded stiffly.

The terse answer did not bother Ethan or Gen. They just wanted to look at the magnificent fossil one more time before the hordes descended. The lighting was perfect.

"It really looks like a miracle," Gen said. "Even with the guard."

Ethan smiled at her. He knew how she felt about the guard. All along, Gen had been opposed to the hiring of a security guard, much less an armed security guard. For weeks she lobbied Ethan and Abi to convince Dr. Emery to drop his plans for a guard. In her mind, a security guard made the fossil seem inaccessible to the people.

Abi and Ethan agreed, however, that the need for security was obvious. To relic hunters, the Hobbs Point Fossil would be a real prize, easily one of the most valuable artifacts in existence. Any number of collectors would love to get their hands on it. Also, no one was completely convinced that Frost and whoever hired him had completely lost interest. For those reasons, Abigail insisted that the fossil be contained in a one-inch-thick, bulletproof acrylic case. Dr. Emery wanted more than that. Initially, he argued long and hard that they should display a replica, maintaining that displaying the original was far too risky. The only way he would agree with its public display was if the fossil would be guarded by an armed security officer.

Gen was unhappy, but in the end realized she had to be realistic. Ethan thought the presence of the armed guard made the display more impressive, not that it wasn't impressive enough. Of course, he also thought laser beams would be even better.

"You know, we won't have it forever," Gen said, gazing at the fossil.

Ethan looked at her and once again was confused by what she meant. "Umm, do you want to explain that?"

"Someday it will be gone," she said. "I wish it were not true, but I'm afraid it is. We can't protect it forever. In the end, maybe that's not so bad. We are meant to live by faith."

Ethan smiled. He was beginning to understand what Gen was talking about. This was starting to get interesting.

"This place is going to be packed soon, Ethan. Before the doors open, I would love to get a picture of you posing with the new exhibit, fighting the dinosaur with all the hunters."

"I can do that," Ethan said.

Ethan stood at the front of the exhibit so Gen could get an awesome photo.

"He kinda looks like you," Gen said.

"The dinosaur?" Ethan asked with a grin. "Oh, you must mean this dude here in front with the spear. It was my dream, you know. He *should* look like me."

"I never knew you were so hairy," Gen said. "OK, pick up one of the spears lying on the floor and pretend like you're going to throw it at the allosaurus."

"Like this?"

"No, no! Hold it like you mean business," Gen said. "You're trying to kill it with that spear, not clean his teeth."

Ethan assumed a more primal pose. "How's this?"

∞ ∞ ∞ ∞ ∞ ∞ ∞

Back outside, Sterner Broadcasting's science correspondent was entertaining the crowd waiting to get in. Abi had everyone's full attention. "All right, I have a trivia question. The first person shouting out the correct answer will get to see the exhibit with our camera crew. That's in just five minutes! Are you ready for the question?"

A loud cheer from the crowd was followed by complete silence as the museum visitors waited for the question.

"OK, you all know that the dinosaur bone was pierced by a spear. Who can tell me what the spearhead is made from?"

Immediately, someone from the crowd shouted, "Obsidian! Obsidian!"

"That's right," Abi said. "Whoever shouted that answer, come on up. We are ready to go inside."

Abigail held the microphone away from her mouth as a smiling man bound up the stairs and stood next to her.

"Joseph Nori: that really wasn't fair."

"Yes, it was fair," Joseph said excitedly. "I was the first to answer. Now let's go in."

∞ ∞ ∞ ∞ ∞ ∞ ∞

Still posing with his spear, Ethan looked up as the front doors opened. A small group marched into the foyer: one cameraman, one person holding a bright light, his mother, and Joseph. *How in the world did Joseph pull that off?* Ethan beamed at his mother, microphone in hand, as she began telling the world about the remarkable discovery.

The commotion in the foyer was suddenly overshadowed by a loud crash. Ethan turned toward the exhibit room in time to see the acrylic case bouncing across the marble floor.

Dr. Emery was shouting, "The fossil! He's got the fossil! Someone stop him!"

The security guard was sprinting out of the room with the fossil tucked under his arm. On instinct, Ethan tightly gripped the spear he had just been posing with, coiled his body like a spring, and took dead aim.

Gen gasped. "Ethan—no!"

Ethan's arm shot forward like a whip; the spear sliced through the air.

The "security guard" never knew what hit him. The spear stabbed deeply into the wall, about knee high. The guard hit the protruding shaft at full speed, nearly achieving a full frontal flip, but landing flat on his back while still clutching the fossil.

Joseph, in an unexpected display of courage, sprinted to the downed thief and snatched the fossil from his grasp.

"That belongs to the museum," Joseph said defiantly, standing over the man.

Unfortunately, the guard was able to quickly regain his bearings. He jumped to his feet and sprinted through the exit before anyone could stop him.

Joseph looked back at Ethan. "That was one amazing throw!"

"What do you mean?" Ethan asked. "I missed."

"I expected this would happen," Dr. Emery said. "What do we do now? We should call the police, but we were supposed to open in a few minutes."

"And we will," Ethan said. "Those doors will open in a few minutes, and all those people are going to see the Hobbs Point Fossil. Heck, the police can see it too."

Gen smiled at him. "Ethan's right. We still have the fossil—for now. We're not going to let a little bit of evil prevent a whole lot of people from seeing the truth."

The Hobbs Point Fossil was replaced on its pedestal. The undamaged acrylic case was set back on top. Dr. Emery relocked the case, although at this point, it seemed a futile gesture.

The doors opened exactly at nine. Eighty-five hundred people saw the Hobbs Point Fossil with their own eyes that day.

Eighty-five hundred people saw the truth.

∞ ∞ ∞ ∞ ∞ ∞ ∞

Later that evening, a small group of people gathered at Abigail Booker's home to celebrate. Gen and Raymond brought cookies and popcorn balls. David brought Hot Pockets. Ethan and Dr. Emery were busy in the kitchen making caveman drawings on crackers with Cheez Whiz. Ethan's Aunt Shelly looked beautiful but overdressed for the party as she mixed up some punch.

David walked up to Ethan. "Son, could I talk to you for a minute?"

"I don't know, Dad. Me and the professor are kinda on a roll with my cave paintings," Ethan said with a grin. "Of course. Let's head to the garage."

Father and son walked out to the garage and leaned against the Monte Carlo. David started. "I don't know if your mother told you yet, but I asked her to marry me again."

Ethan smiled. Not that many months earlier, Ethan would have been horrified by the thought. Now he understood, completely, that people can change.

"I think that's great, Dad. When will this happen?"

"I don't know. She didn't say yes. Of course, she didn't say no, either. I do think it will happen. She said she just needed a bit more time."

"How much time?" Ethan asked.

"It doesn't matter. What does matter is . . ." David's voice broke.

"What is it, Dad?"

Ethan's father took a deep breath. "What does matter is that she forgave me. It seems impossible. After what I have done to her, to you. Forgiveness is something that I absolutely do not deserve. But she did it anyway. Can you believe that?"

"Yeah, I'm starting to believe a lot of things that I never thought were possible," Ethan answered. He gave his dad a hug, a real hug, with a couple of manly thumps on the back. "Let's get back inside," Ethan said.

Gen was waiting for Ethan. "I'm guessing you two had a nice chat."

"Oh, I don't know," Ethan said. "We just talked about cars and baseball and stuff."

Gen smiled and kissed him. "Cars—and stuff. Be sure to tell me about the stuff later."

The doorbell rang. Raymond was the first to the door. "Joseph, you're late for the party."

Joseph blushed. He was all dressed up and clutched a small bouquet of daisies in his fist. "I am not here for a party. Is Miss Shelly here? We have a date."

"A date? You?" Raymond said.

Shelly walked around the corner. "Good evening, Mr. Nori. I'm ready."

All Joseph could say was, "Goodness gracious."

"No one goes anywhere yet," Abigail said. "There's something I would like all of you to watch on TV. It's time for the news."

The group crowded around the television. Abi turned the channel to the Sterner Broadcasting Network, of course. A familiar face sat behind the anchor desk.

"Good evening. This is Ian Walters."

"Hey, Ian's moving up in the world," Raymond said.

"Tonight, we have exclusive footage from the Seattle Museum of Natural History. Our own Dr. Abigail Booker was on hand for an amazing scene."

The scene switched to Abi, microphone in hand, entering the museum with Joseph. "And here we are, one half hour before the grand opening—"

She stopped speaking as Dr. Emery suddenly shouted, off camera: "He's got the fossil. Someone stop him!"

The camera swung around to the source of the commotion. A man dressed as a security guard, carrying something under his arm, ran past the new exhibit. There was Ethan, unleashing his spear. The camera captured the scene perfectly. The spear missed the guard by inches before imbedding itself in the wall. Everyone in the group winced as the thief hit the spear hard with one knee, flipped, and landed hard on his back. Joseph arrived quickly, heroically snatching the fossil from his grasp. This was great television.

Having recorded the news report, the group replayed the scene at least twenty more times. Raymond started adding color commentary: ". . . and the security guard has failed to complete this round of the limbo contest!" The small group enjoyed reliving the experience over and over.

After about the twentieth viewing, Gen said, "Next time, we may not be so fortunate. The thief did get away. We have no idea who was behind this. So do you think they will try again?"

"Of course they will," Ethan said. "Someday they will succeed. Dr. Emery could install laser beams, but it won't matter. Someday the fossil will be gone."

"Ethan's right," Gen said. "The truth is always under attack. Always has been, always will be."

"That's really discouraging," Joseph said.

"No, it's really OK, Joseph," Ethan said. "Think what we have learned. We shouldn't need to have proof in order to understand the truth. I just read in the Bible: 'Know the truth, and the truth will set you free.' Sure, someday the fossil will be gone. I don't think we were meant to have it forever. But I think that's what faith is all about."

"That works for some people," Abi said. "Faith is so hard that many people just find it easier to believe the lie."

The group was quiet. So many things to think about.

Meanwhile, Joseph and Shelly had quietly slipped to the front door and out into the night.

Raymond broke the mood. "Let's watch Ethan throw the spear one more time. Maybe this time he'll hit him." Everyone laughed.

Ethan smiled at Gen.

"Life is good," he said. "I can't wait to see what's next."

WHY THE BEHEMOTH MATTERS

Will we ever find a spearhead imbedded in the fossilized bone of a dinosaur?

Before we answer that question, we need to look at modern paleontology. Currently, scientists are confronted with a new and surprising problem. Technology has revealed evidence of soft tissue, blood vessels, and even DNA in fossils that they themselves have dated to be more than fifty million years old. The lifespan of DNA alone is measured in thousands of years, not millions. These and other recent findings support the biblical record of creation.

Why haven't we heard more about this?

Here is the explanation, and it is a large—you might even say behemoth-sized—one.

In the story we just read, there are two behemoths. They are different giants, but both are very real.

One behemoth is described in the book of Job. It is one of the most detailed descriptions of an animal in the Bible. No, it is not a hippo, nor is it an elephant, as many scholars suggest. The "tail . . . like a cedar" rejects that claim. And yes, the cedar tree during the time of Job was a massive, thick tree. This is not poetic language. In the Bible, God's inspired Word, He is not referring to a mythological beast. The Bible is clearly describing a great land animal similar to some well-known and well-documented dinosaurs. The brontosaurus was a gigantic plant eater with great muscles and very strong bones. Yes, it had a tail like a cedar. And there would be no need for this creature to be alarmed when the river raged, as one description puts it, in the Bible. These beasts were huge.

Yet many of us don't know what to do with this passage. We have become so brainwashed by the popularized teachings of evolution that we believe it is not possible that mankind once lived in the same world as dinosaurs. We have compromised our understanding of Scripture in order to present ourselves with a more acceptable worldview.

Which leads us to another behemoth.

This behemoth is an incredibly powerful collection of professors, scientists, politicians, celebrities, teachers, and others who scoff at Christian believers when we profess that God is the creator. They scoff when we tell them that life has meaning, that we are significant. This massive cultural behemoth also tempts us with the idea of life without an ultimate judge—a life with shades of gray, where we alone determine what is right or wrong. This behemoth inflicts a worldly view of life by random chance and inevitable, inescapable death. Somehow this behemoth convinces us that being intellectual is superior to our understanding of God. For many of us, it is our desire, our treasure, to be thought of as enlightened. We hate being laughed at. We hate being . . . persecuted. It is easier these days to possess a worldview regarding evolution. We treasure being intellectual.

Was the beast described in Job a brontosaurus? Is this an issue of salvation?

Unfortunately, Christians will argue points such as these with one another. They will fight over the evidence of a "young earth" or an "old earth." This topic has polarized many of us and has led to dangerous stone throwing.

On the topic of creation, we need to be united, not divided. There is unlimited value in study, debate, and fellowship on this issue. It is far better to be engaged than to be entrenched.

This issue is a challenging one for me, and I pray that it is challenging for you as well. But it is far better for Scripture to prove challenging for us than it is to simply discard it.

So then, will we ever find a spearhead imbedded in the fossilized bone of a dinosaur?

It is very possible that we already have.

John Ingelin
Andover, Minnesota
March 2015

ENDNOTES

1. George Orwell. Quoted in *Intelligent Intervention*, by Robert Steven Thomas (Indianapolis, IN: Dog Ear Publishing, 2011), 1.

2. C. S. Lewis, *God in the Dock: Essays on Theology and Ethics* (Grand Rapids, MI: Eerdmans Publishing Company, 1970), [page number]. © Trustees of the estate of C. S. Lewis, 32.

3. Malcolm Bowden quoting Charles Darwin, *True Science Agrees with the Bible* (London: Sovereign Publications, 1998), 43.

4. "Irrepressible Churchill: A Treasury of Winston Churchill's Wit," in *Reader's Digest*, Vol. 40 (Cleveland, OH: World Publishing Company, 1942), 52.

5. William B. Provine, "Evolution: Free Will and Punishment and Meaning in Life." (information taken from a slide presented in Provine's "Darwin Day" address, University of Tennessee-Knoxville, 1998), 74.

6. William Shenstone, "William Shenstone Quotes," Quotes.net, STANDS 4 LLC, 2015, accessed March 10, 2015, http://www.quotes.net/quote/43688, 6.

7. C. S. Lewis, *The Abolition of Man* (San Francisco: Harper One, March 2009), 105.

8. C. S. Lewis, *The Problem of Pain* (San Francisco: Harper One, March 2009), 112.

9. John Locke, *Essay Concerning Human Understanding* (Amherst, NY: Prometheus Books, 1995), 123.

10. Felix Adler, *The Essentials of Spirituality* (New York: James Pott and Co., 1908), 129.

11. Soren Kierkegaard, *Works of Love* (New York: Harper Perennial, 1962), 137.

12. Martin Luther King Jr. (in his acceptance speech for the Nobel Prize, Oslo, Norway, December 10, 1964), 152.

13. Soren Kierkegaard, *The Journals of Soren Kierkegaard* (Oxford, UK: Oxford University Press, 1840), 161.

14. D. Elton Trueblood, *Basic Christianity: Addresses of D. Elton Trueblood* (Richmond, IN: Friends United Press, 1977), 171.